Jane Austen's

Northanger Abbey

AWESOMELY AUSTEN

Illustrated by Églantine Ceulemans

Pride and Prejudice – Katherine Woodfine

Emma – Katy Birchall

Persuasion – Narinder Dhami

Sense and Sensibility – Joanna Nadin

Mansfield Park – Ayisha Malik

Northanger Abbey – Steven Butler

Jane Austen's

NORTHANGER ABBEY

RETOLD BY STEVEN BUTLER

ILLUSTRATED BY ÉGLANTINE CEULEMANS

HODDER CHILDREN'S BOOKS

First published in Great Britain in 2020 by Hodder & Stoughton

1 3 5 7 9 10 8 6 4 2

All characters and events in this publication, other than those clearly in the public domain, are fictitious and any resemblance to real persons, living or dead, is purely coincidental.

A CIP catalogue record for this book is available from the British Library.

ISBN 978 1 444 95069 4

Typeset in Bembo by Hewer Text UK Ltd, Edinburgh
Printed and bound in Great Britain by Clays Ltd, Elcograf S.p.A

The paper and board used in this book are made from wood from responsible sources.

Hodder Children's Books
An imprint of
Hachette Children's Group
Part of Hodder & Stoughton
Carmelite House
50 Victoria Embankment
London, EC4Y 0DZ

An Hachette UK Company
www.hachette.co.uk

www.hachettechildrens.co.uk

Northanger Abbey, by Jane Austen, was first published in 1817.

This was the Regency era – a time when English society was sharply divided by wealth and women were expected to marry young.

The heroine of this story, Catherine, might have some things in common with modern readers, but she lived in a very different world.

You can find out more about Jane Austen and what England was like in 1817 at the back of this book!

MAIN CHARACTERS

MR MORLAND

Father of ten children. Mr Morland is a respectable clergyman.

MRS MORLAND

Mother of ten children. Mrs Morland is a friendly and kind-hearted woman.

JAMES MORLAND

Catherine's affectionate older brother. James studies at Oxford University.

CATHERINE MORLAND

Our heroine! Catherine has nine siblings but is closest to James. She loves reading and has an overactive imagination that sometimes gets her into trouble.

MR ALLEN

A wealthy family friend of the Morlands. Mr Allen is fond of eating and playing cards.

MRS ALLEN

A wealthy family friend of the Morlands. Mrs Allen is good-natured but cares more about fashion than anything else.

MRS THORPE

An old school friend of Mrs Allen.
Mrs Thorpe has one son and three daughters.

JOHN THORPE

Mrs Thorpe's son. John is a short, rude and self-centred man. He is a university friend of James Morland.

ISABELLA THORPE

The eldest of Mrs Thorpe's daughters. Isabella is attractive and lively but loves to gossip and enjoys having all eyes on her.

ANNE AND MARIA THORPE

Mrs Thorpe's two younger daughters.

GENERAL TILNEY
A tall, handsome but intimidating man. General Tilney expects his children to marry into wealth.
MRS TILNEY
Mrs Tilney dies before the start of the novel. She is described as a beautiful and caring woman.
CAPTAIN FREDERICK TILNEY
The eldest of the Tilney siblings, Frederick is a captain in the navy. He is a mischievous and selfish man.
HENRY TILNEY
A charming and intelligent man, Henry is the parson of a small village. He immediately catches Catherine's attention.
ELEANOR TILNEY
The youngest of the Tilney siblings, Eleanor is a shy but sweet woman. She has a lot in common with Catherine.

CHAPTER ONE

If you had met Catherine Morland when she was young, my dear reader, you wouldn't think in a million years that she might one day grow up to become the heroine of her own strange and exciting story.

She lived a long time ago in the days when little girls were expected to be prim and delicate and could be found skipping, playing with dolls, tying their plaits up with ribbons or gathering flowers. But Catherine didn't enjoy any of those things. She wasn't dainty or polite and was far more likely to be mistaken as a wild creature than the daughter of a respectable clergyman.

Maybe it was because Catherine had three older brothers as playmates that she much preferred joining in with their noisy games instead. And since Mr and Mrs Morland were happy for her to rough and tumble around with her siblings, Catherine spent her days rampaging with dirt-stained dresses and knotty, unbrushed hair.

No one could beat Catherine at a game of cricket.

She climbed trees faster than a startled squirrel, always yawned her way through schoolwork or piano lessons, and if she ever occasionally showed an interest in picking flowers, it was usually only because her mother had told her not to.

Curiosity and mischief ran through her veins, but, despite all this, she was a kind, well-natured child with a good heart.

By the time Catherine turned fifteen, the scruffy wildling who once rolled down hills and hid at bathtime had started to slowly vanish before everyone's eyes.

Her mother had given birth to another six children by then, and though Catherine still loved to chase and play ball with her nine brothers and sisters, she was showing signs of turning into a . . . a . . . POLITE YOUNG WOMAN!?

It was on a sunny afternoon, while Mr and Mrs Morland were happily watching their children playing in the sunny gardens of their home in Fullerton, that Mrs Morland remarked, 'Catherine is improving. She's becoming quite a respectable young lady – she looks lovely today.'

And Mrs Morland was right. Catherine's thin, awkward frame had softened with plumpness as she'd aged. She'd begun to curl her once lank hair and dressed neatly for a change. Her love of dirt had given way to a yearning for finery and alongside these little improvements, Catherine had grown smarter.

For as long as she could remember, books had always been of absolutely no interest. They were long and boring and filled with all sorts of information that Catherine simply didn't care about.

But . . . at the age of fifteen, she discovered novels! Wonderful, heart-stopping novels filled with stories of brave heroines and their witty escapades in high society.

Catherine's heart was gripped in the turning of a page, making her a greedy reader in mere moments – longing for the excitement of faraway places, danger-filled escapes from dastardly villains and dancing at the grandest of parties. She couldn't put them down.

By the time Catherine was seventeen, she had read practically every novel she could find in the county of Wiltshire, but even with her wildly growing imagination, she couldn't have predicted the marvellous things that were about to happen to her.

Catherine Morland was soon to become a heroine like the ones in her beloved stories . . . she just didn't know it yet.

CHAPTER TWO

'Too much wine and cheese,' Mrs Allen sighed, shaking her head at her husband's round belly. 'And not enough exercise!'

The day had arrived when Catherine was to begin her journey to becoming a heroine, and she was sitting in the parlour with her mother and father, chatting with wealthy friends of the family, Mr and Mrs Allen.

'The doctor says I have gout,' Mr Allen grumbled over his cup of tea.

'He's very gouty,' Mrs Allen agreed. 'Full of it.'

'So, we are off for a stay in Bath,' continued Mr

Allen, scowling at his wife. 'The doctors are sure the waters from the hot spring, fine air and a spot of relaxation will sort it out in a jiffy.'

'And,' Mrs Allen continued with a twinkle of excitement in her eyes, 'we wondered if young Catherine would like to join us for a time?'

That was that . . . Catherine was to accompany the Allens to their lodgings in Bath. In what seemed like seconds the plan was made, and she hurried about the house, packing away a few books and the nicer dresses from her wardrobe. Mr and Mrs Morland were completely delighted that their daughter would be properly introduced to high society and agreed to it all at once.

Catherine could barely contain her happiness – she was going to get her first taste of real adventure. She struggled to stop herself from grinning as thoughts of coach rides and beautiful tea rooms and candlelit balls waltzed through her head.

'Now, Catherine, my darling,' Mrs Morland said with wide eyes as the hour of departure grew near, 'you must take care.'

Any other mother would have warned her daughter to be wary of potential dangers, or untrustworthy barons, or bad people who might do Catherine harm, but Mrs Morland knew almost nothing about life outside the sleepy village of Fullerton, so she simply told her to wear a scarf in the evenings and not to spend too much money.

Spend too much money?!? There wasn't any chance of that. Mr Morland, being very sensible, only gave his daughter ten guineas. Catherine didn't mind, though. She was completely swept up in the wonder of being whisked away to beautiful, magical Bath.

There were kisses and hugs and a few emotional sobs from Mrs Morland as their daughter waved farewell through the coach window, but the journey began without any further hitches. And as the horses pulled the three holidaymakers swiftly along country lanes, Catherine half expected them to come across cut-throat robbers or be blown away in some dreadful storm, but there was no such disaster like the ones she read about in her novels.

The most dramatic thing to happen in the entire journey was Mrs Allen worrying that she'd left her clogs at an inn they'd stopped at, but even that turned out to be a false alarm.

For most of the sleepy journey, Catherine gazed dreamily out of the window, or she quietly examined Mr and Mrs Allen as they dozed and chatted.

Mr Allen was all bulging belly and red nose, while Mrs Allen was altogether more lovely. She wasn't particularly beautiful, or clever, or accomplished in any way, but she had a good nature about her that made Catherine smile and look forward to the weeks ahead.

By the time they reached Bath, she was practically fizzing with delight. Catherine watched as the coach rolled along wide boulevards and grand crescents, bustling with the most fashionable people she'd ever seen. There were shops and theatres, stately homes and clamorous concert halls, and all of it looked marvellous.

'Here we are,' Mr Allen grunted as he stepped on to the pavement, before turning to help his wife and their young guest climb down after him. 'Home away from home.'

They'd arrived on Pulteney Street, where Mr Allen had rented comfortable lodgings in a small but neatly appointed hotel. Trunks and cases were off-loaded from the coach, rooms were explored and bedchambers were allocated, but Catherine barely had time to unpack her books before Mrs Allen whisked her out into the busy street.

'There's so much to do!' She beamed with a look of startled glee as she ushered Catherine in the direction of the most glamorous shops in town. 'I want to go everywhere and see everything!'

Mrs Allen seemed more enthusiastic about their arrival in Bath than Catherine was, and it only made her all the more likeable. The fussing woman had a delightful passion for fine things and expensive clothing was her absolute favourite.

'Look at this one, Catherine!' she cooed, twirling about a cramped shop like a giddy rooster with a new feather bonnet perched on her head. 'I feel like a queen!'

The afternoon was spent hurrying from one fancy boutique to another, Catherine buying a few pretty gowns with the little money she had, while Mrs Allen grabbed any item of the latest fashion that she could get her hands on.

Catherine had her hair cut and styled by the best hand, and that evening, after dressing with great care and attention to the tiniest of details, Mrs Allen and her maid declared she looked just right.

With such friendly encouragement, Catherine felt certain she could attend her first ever ball and no one would be able to tell she was secretly not of high society . . . not even close. A tingle of anticipation crept up her spine and made her shiver with nervous excitement.

Unfortunately, it took Mrs Allen so long to get

ready that they were already late for the party before she'd even wobbled her way downstairs in her newest gown of lace and pearls. And by the time they had reached the Bath Assembly Rooms where the ball was taking place, it was teeming with noisily chattering revellers.

Mr Allen quickly made his excuses and headed straight for the card room, leaving Catherine and Mrs Allen to face the jostling mob by themselves. There was a densely packed crowd of men by the door and Mrs Allen cautiously led the way through them, caring far more about her dress than for her young guest.

Once inside the candlelit hall, Catherine was shocked to find the entire room was just as busy. Everywhere she turned, groups of people packed the space. All she could see of the dancers were a few high feathers bobbing on the tops of ladies' heads somewhere near the centre of the floor. And the further in they got, the more Catherine felt awkward and very alone. Before long, they found themselves squashed into a corner at the far end of the hall, with no one to talk to or notice them.

'I wish you could dance, my dear,' Mrs Allen repeatedly sighed as she searched the throng for a familiar face. It seemed she too had started to realise they didn't know anyone at all. 'I wish you could find a partner.'

At first, Catherine nodded and agreed every time Mrs Allen mumbled this. After all, now they were inside the ballroom, she longed to be one of the delicate ladies gliding around the floor with a handsome partner. But it soon became irritating, and Catherine was glad when the bell invited everyone to head downstairs to the tea room.

She couldn't help but feel disappointed as they began squeezing out of the hall the same way they'd squeezed in earlier that evening. Being nudged and pushed this way and that like she was invisible had grown tiring, and although Catherine certainly didn't depend on the attention of the young men all around her, she wouldn't have minded the tiniest bit of admiration from them. In any case, she had dressed up for the occasion and was looking just as neat and dainty as all the other young ladies.

'How uncomfortable it is,' Catherine whispered as they sat down at a long table of sour-faced guests, 'not to have a single friend here.'

'Yes, my dear,' Mrs Allen replied, smiling absent-mindedly. 'It's extremely uncomfortable.'

'What shall we do? The people at this table don't look very pleased to see us sitting with them. We're forcing ourselves into their party.'

'You're right,' Mrs Allen agreed. 'I wish we had friends here at the ball for us to sit with.'

'I wish we had even a single friend . . . it would be someone for us to talk to.'

'Quite true,' Mrs Allen sighed again with a shrug of her shoulders. 'And then I could find you a dance partner . . . and . . . umm . . .' She became distracted by a woman walking past and started wrinkling her nose and mumbling about how old-fashioned the lady's dress was.

It was no use. Catherine and Mrs Allen ended up sitting quietly, sipping tea and talking to no one, until Mr Allen finally joined them from the card room at the end of the night.

'Well, Miss Morland,' he said, brushing crumbs from the front of his waistcoat, 'I hope you have enjoyed your first ball.'

'It was wonderful,' she lied, trying to hide a yawn.

'But no one danced with her,' Mrs Allen whined. 'I wish we could have found Catherine a partner.'

'There will be lots more balls,' Mr Allen comforted his wife. 'We shall do better another evening.' He smiled at Catherine and she tried to smile back, feeling certain that Mr Allen was wrong.

But . . . as they made their way to leave, Catherine overheard two scrawny young men comment on how pretty she looked, and though she hated to admit it, the entire evening suddenly didn't seem quite so dreadful after all.

CHAPTER THREE

The days in Bath quickly fell into a repetitive pattern as, every morning, Catherine and Mrs Allen would go about their regular routine together. There were always shops to call into, concerts to attend and some new part of the town to be explored. And they never failed to visit the Grand Pump Room, a lavish meeting place where people could dance, sip tea and listen to musicians playing beautiful waltzes.

Every lunchtime, Mrs Allen would parade nosily up and down the Grand Pump Room's largest hall to see who was about, smiling and wafting her fan, but secretly still moaning that she wished they had friends in Bath. Catherine would cringe to herself as they walked back and forth, looking at everybody but speaking to no one, wondering if her holiday was actually just a terrible mistake. How could they know nobody at all?

Fortune finally smiled on our young heroine, however, when she made an appearance at one of the less formal daytime balls. The host spotted Catherine in her pretty muslin dress with blue trimmings and quickly paired her with her first living and breathing dance partner. Catherine couldn't believe her luck!

The young man went by the name of Henry Tilney, and although she didn't know many gentlemen, Catherine felt sure that he just might be one. Henry was tall and fairly handsome, had an intelligence about him, and Catherine guessed he was probably about five or six years older than her. She suddenly felt very lucky indeed to be partnered

with someone so lively and pleasing as he guided her around the floor.

There was barely a chance to talk while they were dancing, but after the quartet had stopped playing and they took their seats for tea, Catherine found Henry to be very funny and playful.

'I have been a dreadful partner,' he pretend-sobbed with a look of mischief in his eye.

'Why?' Catherine asked.

'I haven't asked you any of the *terribly important* questions a partner *has* to ask. Can you ever forgive me for being so neglectful?'

Catherine couldn't stifle her giggle. Could Henry also be someone who thought the rules of high society seemed a little . . . she could barely bring herself to think it . . . stupid?

'I shall ask all of them now at once!' he said,

pretending to be unbelievably serious and fascinated. 'Have you been in Bath for long?'

'About a week,' Catherine answered, trying not to laugh.

'Incredible!' he gasped with joke astonishment. 'Have you been to the Bath Assembly Rooms?'

'Yes, sir, I was there on Monday.'

'Have you been to the theatre?'

'Yes, I saw the play on Tuesday.'

'To the concert?'

'Yes, sir, on Wednesday.'

'And are you pleased with Bath?' Henry asked, looking painfully concerned.

'I like it very much,' Catherine said. She thought his playfulness was wonderful after all the grim-faced guests at the ball.

'And now I must smile with huge relief and we can have a normal conversation,' Henry chuckled.

Catherine turned her head away, trying to hide another laugh.

'I can see what you think of me,' he said gravely. 'You're going to write terrible things about me in your journal.'

'My journal!' Catherine huffed, joining in with Henry's game.

'Yes! You're going to write that you went to a ball and was bothered by a strange half-witted man who made you dance and distressed you with his nonsense.'

'No, I won't!' Catherine actually laughed out loud this time.

'But I'll tell you what you should be writing,' Henry continued. 'You should write that you met a marvellous young man, had brilliant conversations – he seems like a genius – and that you hope to know much more about him. *That* is what I *hope* you'll write.'

Catherine opened her mouth to speak, but she was interrupted as Mrs Allen bustled over, scrabbling with something on the sleeve of her latest enormous dress.

'My dear Catherine,' she squawked. 'Please help me with this pin in my sleeve. I think it has torn a hole! I'll be so upset if it has!'

Catherine stood to help Mrs Allen, but Henry stepped in before she reached her chaperone.

'This is a very fine muslin gown,' He said, carefully pulling out the rogue pin.

'Do you know about dresses, sir?' Mrs Allen asked.

'I know all about muslin and such.' He smiled. 'I buy my own neckties and often help my sister with choosing what to buy.'

The grin that spread across Mrs Allen's face said she was extremely impressed with Mr Tilney's knowledge.

'Sadly, there aren't many shops where I live,' Henry continued. 'My family home is out in the countryside . . . here in Bath the boutiques are quite lovely, though.'

But Mrs Allen had stopped listening, still

gawping and fanning herself that a gentleman knew about fine fabrics. She turned to Catherine when Henry's back was turned for a moment and mouthed the words 'HE'S WONDERFUL!'.

Catherine danced with Mr Tilney one more time, once Mrs Allen had stopped jabbering on about muslins and silks, and when the music finally ended, she felt a definite desire to see this strange young man again.

In the evening, as she climbed into bed, Catherine thought of Henry once more. Mr Allen had told her earlier that day that he knew of Mr Tilney. He was a very respectable clergyman, just like her father, and he was from a wealthy family in Gloucestershire.

No one knows if Catherine dreamed of her new dance partner that night. But if she did, she certainly didn't write it down in her journal . . .

The next morning, Catherine hurried to the Grand Pump Room with far more eagerness than usual. She was determined to see Mr Tilney again and ready to meet him with a smile. But no smile was necessary – Mr Tilney did not appear.

It seemed like every person in Bath had crammed their way into the building's ornate hall, hurrying up and down the stairs and into the tea rooms. Everyone except Henry. Catherine searched the crowds and felt a stab of disappointment at his absence.

'What a delightful place Bath is,' said Mrs Allen as they sat down after parading around the room until they were tired. 'But I do wish we had friends here.'

Catherine had lost count of how many times her chaperone had grumbled this, and she resisted the urge to groan to herself. She may have even spiralled into a bad mood just then had they not been interrupted by a woman of about Mrs Allen's age, marching up to them with a telling look on her face.

'I cannot be mistaken,' the lady said. 'It's been years since I've had the pleasure of seeing you, but I think I know you!'

'Yes, indeed!' gasped Mrs Allen. 'Your face is terribly familiar.'

Very soon, the two ladies were chattering away, realising that they had been childhood school friends.

The woman's name turned out to be Mrs Thorpe and it only took a matter of seconds before she was telling Mrs Allen all about her three eldest sons and their wonderful achievements.

'John is at Oxford University, Edward is at the Merchant Taylors' School in London and William is at sea,' Mrs Thorpe cooed. 'I'm so proud of them!'

Mrs Allen had no such triumphs to boast about and decided to simply smile and nod sleepily as her old friend talked. Catherine almost felt sorry for Mrs Allen until she noticed her eyeing the lace on Mrs Thorpe's dress and knew she was secretly comparing it to the much finer silk that her own gown was woven from.

'Oh, and here come my dear girls,' cried Mrs Thorpe, pointing at three smartly dressed young women who were walking across the Grand Pump Room towards them, arm in arm.

The Thorpe sisters were introduced one by one, and Mrs Allen introduced Catherine in return.

'Of course!' laughed the eldest daughter, Isabella, as she studied Catherine's face. 'Miss Morland, you look exactly like your brother James.'

For a brief moment, Catherine could hardly hide her surprise. After Mrs Thorpe had recognised Mrs Allen so unexpectedly, she hadn't thought in a million years that her eldest brother's name would pop into the conversation as well. Although she very quickly remembered that James had talked about a dear friend at his college with the surname Thorpe and how he'd spent time with his family last Christmas.

'You're the very picture of him!' Mrs Thorpe joined in with Isabella. 'I'd have known your face anywhere, Miss Morland.'

'That's that,' Isabella said, taking Catherine's arm. 'We simply have to get to know one another better.' And before our heroine could say another word, they were walking a lap of the room together.

Catherine's head was practically swimming with delight at making a friend in Bath, and she almost forgot about Mr Tilney as she and Isabella paraded together, chatting and laughing.

Their conversation quickly turned to the subjects that seemed to be on the mind of practically every young woman in Bath that day – things like dresses, balls and flirting with handsome young men.

Catherine soon noticed that Isabella, being four years older and more than four years wiser, knew a lot more about life in high society than her. She listened as Miss Thorpe compared the balls of Bath to those of Tunbridge and its fashions with the fashions of London. She could spot even the tiniest of flirtatious smiles between a woman and a man on opposite sides of the floor and make quick and witty remarks about anyone they glimpsed through the crowd, even for a second.

It seemed like Isabella possessed new and exciting magical powers, and Catherine couldn't help admiring them.

By the time they had completed six laps of the room and it was time to leave, they had grown so fond of each other that Isabella insisted on walking Catherine all the way back to Mr and Mrs Allen's front door.

'I'll see you at the theatre tonight,' Miss Thorpe said as they shook hands affectionately. 'And in chapel the next morning.'

As Isabella turned to go, Catherine ran inside and up the stairs to watch Miss Thorpe from the drawing room window. She admired her graceful walk, the fashionable style of her figure and dress, and she felt completely grateful and happy for being given the chance to make such a marvellous new friend.

CHAPTER FIVE

Although Catherine was preoccupied with smiling and waving across the theatre to Miss Thorpe that evening, she didn't forget to keep one eye out for Mr Tilney.

Ignoring the actors on stage, she carefully searched each and every seat in turn, but he wasn't there. He *had* mentioned between chuckles and mischievous glances on that happy day earlier in the week that he hated watching plays just as much as he hated the Grand Pump Room.

Catherine hoped for better luck the following morning, and when she woke up to bright sunshine, she felt much happier. Good weather meant that everyone in Bath would be out and about. How could she not bump into Henry Tilney on a day like this?

As soon as chapel was over, Catherine, as well as Mr and Mrs Allen, joined Mrs Thorpe and her daughters. They all visited the Grand Pump Room, but finding there was no one of any interest there, headed across town to the Royal Crescent (the most expensive road in Bath, filled with terrifically ornate houses) where they could mingle and stroll with a far higher class of people.

'Much better,' Mr Allen mumbled to himself as he breathed the fresh air and took in the beautiful arc of buildings. 'This is the finest road in the world. Do you like it, Catherine?'

But now it was Catherine's turn to not listen. She and Isabella, arm in arm, were already deep in conversation and enjoying the fun of their new-found friendship. They talked and giggled about everything they saw, although Catherine

couldn't help but feel secretly disappointed not to spot Henry as they left the Royal Crescent and ambled through the park that spread out below it.

He seemed to have completely vanished. Every time she searched, Mr Tilney was nowhere to be found. He wasn't in any of the morning tea rooms or afternoon concerts, at the evening balls held at the Bath Assembly Rooms, or on any street they ventured along. His name didn't even appear in the Grand Pump Room signature book, and Catherine started to think he must have left Bath altogether and gone back to his family home in Gloucestershire.

'He never mentioned his holiday here would be so short,' Catherine thought out loud, barely noticing that all this mystery was making Henry seem more and more like a hero in one of her exciting novels.

'He sounds very charming,' Isabella said with wide eyes after Catherine told her all about the strange and amusing dance partner. 'You should keep searching.'

Catherine sighed one of the hundreds of sighs that she'd let out over the past few days, and Isabella teased her playfully about it.

As the days passed, their friendship grew

stronger and stronger, and now that Mrs Allen had met Mrs Thorpe and could be found chasing her old school friend all over town like an overeager puppy, the two girls were left to spend as much time together as possible.

They went everywhere and did everything, laughing and chattering as they went. Even on rainy days, they defied the mud and wet and shut themselves indoors as a duo to read novels. Yes, novels . . .

Let's not forget, my dear reader, books are to blame for everything that happens over the next few hundred pages. Just as you are reading this story now, Catherine is so inspired by the heart-stopping adventures she reads in her novels, that she gets herself into all sorts of trouble.

You'll see . . .

CHAPTER SIX

After more than a week of socialising in the day and nights spent at the theatre, the two friends were now at the Grand Pump Room for a morning of tea, gossip and giggling.

Isabella had arrived only five minutes early but grumbled that she had been waiting for at least half an hour when Catherine arrived exactly on time.

'My dearest creature,' she humphed. 'I have been waiting an age!'

They soon hurried to the far end of the room where they could safely watch customers come and go as they chatted about them.

'I bought the prettiest hat you can imagine,' Isabella cooed as they sat down and poured tea. 'You must come and see it at our lodgings later.'

'Of course,' Catherine answered with a smile.

Isabella looked around her and made sure no one could hear them.

'Have you been reading the book I lent you?' she whispered, twitching her eyebrows excitedly. '*The Mysteries of Udolpho*?'

'I've been reading it all morning,' Catherine practically yelped. 'I couldn't put it down. I've read so many novels before but nothing like this – it's perfectly shocking. I've just got to the part with the black veil!'

'Oh! That's a terrifying chapter!'

'You mustn't tell me what's behind the veil,' cried Catherine. 'I'm sure it must be a skeleton. Laurentina's skeleton! I'm delighted with it. If I hadn't been coming here to meet you, I would not have stopped reading for all the world!'

'I'm so glad you like it,' Isabella said.

'I love it!' Catherine replied.

'In that case, when you have finished *Udolpho*, dear creature, we shall read many more novels together. Each one more shocking than the last. I have their titles written down in my pocketbook.'

Isabella pulled out a small notebook and read out loud.

'*The Castle of Wolfenbach*, *The Mysterious Warning*, *The Necromancer*, *The Midnight Bell* . . .'

'They sound horrid!' Catherine laughed.

'They should last us a long time,' said Isabella, just as her face changed. Catherine thought it looked like she had something else to say. 'Do you know, yesterday as you were leaving, I saw a young man looking at you so longingly, I think he is in love with you.'

'Oh, dear,' cried Catherine, blushing. 'How can you say so?'

'It's true, upon my honour, but I know how you feel . . .'

'What do you mean?' asked Catherine warily.

'You don't care about the attention of any other men except your elusive dance partner,' Isabella teased. 'Mr Tilney!'

'I . . . well . . . umm . . .' Catherine could feel herself getting redder and redder. She opened her mouth to speak and was glad when Isabella interrupted her.

'Ugh! Speaking of *other* men. Do you know there are two horrible young men who have been staring at me ever since we sat down?' she said, smoothing her hair and sitting up as primly as she could. 'I'm all they can talk about! Let's move over to the entrance doorway and watch the new arrivals. They won't follow us there.'

With that, the two friends hurried to the far side of the hall, and while Isabella kept her back to the two alarming young men, Catherine was tasked with keeping an eye on them.

'Are they staring?' Isabella kept asking. 'Are they searching for me? I'm certain they will be.'

After a few moments, Catherine reassured her acquaintance not to worry as the youths had left the Grand Pump Room and headed out into the street. She was surprised when Isabella seemed very upset by this.

'Which way did they go?' she moaned. 'One of

them was very handsome.'

'Towards the churchyard.'

'Well, I'm very glad I got rid of them,' Isabella said unconvincingly. 'Now I think we should go outside right away, and I'll show you the pretty hat that I told you about.'

'Shouldn't we wait a minute?' Catherine questioned innocently. 'Otherwise we might bump into the men you wanted to avoid . . .'

'Let's go,' Isabella blurted, and the two set off immediately – Isabella walking as fast as she could in pursuit of the two young men.

CHAPTER SEVEN

In barely a minute, Catherine and Isabella had dashed out of the Grand Pump Room and through the archway on to Cheap Street.

'They're getting away,' Isabella moaned, pointing to the young men, who were already on the other side of the street, vanishing round a corner. 'We'll never catch them now.' And she was right . . .

This late in the morning, Cheap Street was always extremely busy with carts and stagecoaches and huge gaggles of ladies dashing about town in search of pastries, hats and (like Catherine and Isabella) handsome young men.

They were both about to step out into the road but were stopped in their tracks by a speedily approaching horse-drawn carriage.

'Oh, this ghastly traffic,' Isabella said, looking up. 'I detest it!' But her sudden anger was cut very short when she noticed the two people sitting in the fast, little carriage as it whizzed along the street.

'DELIGHTFUL!' she cheered. 'It's our brothers. Look!'

Catherine glanced up and gasped to see her brother, James Morland, sitting next to a stout fellow who looked just like Isabella.

The horse and carriage soon pulled over to the pavement, and the two men climbed down.

'Catherine!' James beamed. He threw his arms round his little sister and hugged her tightly. 'How wonderful.'

'You came all this way to see me?' Catherine laughed. She was so happy at her brother's unexpected arrival that she failed to notice when James turned and nodded a very enthusiastic hello to Isabella, blushing and shuffling his feet about as he did so.

Had she known anything about flirting or love, Catherine would have been able to tell that James was clearly smitten with Isabella, but she didn't . . . so she went on happily believing he'd come all the way to Bath just for her.

'You must meet my brother, John,' said Isabella, guiding Catherine over to the stout gentleman who'd been driving. He was short and ungraceful and had an extremely plain face.

'What do you think of my carriage, Miss Morland,' John grunted as the girls approached him.

'I like it very much,' Catherine said politely, although she secretly didn't know anything about such things.

'And my horse?' John continued without so much as a hello. 'Did you ever see an animal so made for speed in your life?'

Catherine shook her head.

'Fastest horse around. We've done over twenty-five miles with her this morning.' He waggled his eyebrows, clearly thinking that Catherine should be wowed.

When she did open her mouth to respond, John practically ignored her, going on to point out in detail all the *extremely* impressive features of his little carriage. And when the list of seats, trunks, splashing-boards, lamps and silver mouldings was over, he finally asked the two ladies where they were heading.

'We're going back to our lodgings to see mother, and I want to show Catherine my new hat,' Isabella answered her brother.

'That's sorted then,' John barked, offering Catherine his arm. 'Come on, James. We'll walk you both there.'

James and Isabella led the way along the pavement, giggling and whispering as they went.

Isabella was so happy with James's wonderful

company (he was her brother's friend and her friend's brother after all) that when they finally caught up with and passed the two young men she'd been chasing earlier, she only turned round to glance and smile at them three times.

Behind them, Catherine walked and listened as John gabbled about his horse again.

'Do you like open-topped carriages, Miss Morland?'

'I've never been in one.'

'Well, that's settled it,' John cried. 'I shall take you for a ride every day. Tomorrow we'll see the countryside together!'

'Thank you,' Catherine replied with a mixture of excitement and worry. A day trip speeding around the hilly lanes sounded marvellous, but she wasn't sure John would be the greatest company.

She thought for a moment . . .

'Have you ever read *The Mysteries of Udolpho*, Mr Thorpe?'

'*Udolpho*!?! John scoffed. 'I never read novels; I have more important things to do. Novels are full of nonsense! They are the stupidest things in creation.'

Catherine felt ashamed and embarrassed that she'd even bothered to ask. She was thinking about apologising for the question, but they had completed their short walk and had arrived at the Thorpes' lodgings in Edgar Buildings, so it would have to wait.

'Mother! How do you do?' John blurted when Mrs Thorpe appeared at the door. 'Where did you get that dreadful hat? It makes you look like an old witch!'

They were all welcomed inside, and Catherine quietly watched as John paraded around the house, greeting Isabella's two other sisters and telling them they both looked very ugly.

If he had not been her best friend's brother and her brother's best friend, Catherine would have judged John very badly at that moment. She didn't like his manners and found him rude and unpleasant but was stopped mid-thought. Isabella dragged her off to see the new hat and quietly reassured her that John thought she was quite beautiful and wanted to be her dance partner at the ball that night.

'Me?' Catherine whispered, blushing bright red. 'Really?'

'He thinks you're charming,' Isabella giggled. 'He wants to accompany you this evening.'

Catherine may have thought John was a bit of a brute, but she was still young and inexperienced enough to forget all of that and be completely thrilled that someone found her charming and wanted her for a dance partner at the ball. An irritating partner is better than none!

Later that day, after they'd sat and listened to John blustering on for over an hour, James and Catherine said their farewells to the Thorpe family and set off in the direction of Mr and Mrs Allen's lodgings.

'What do you think of my friend?' James asked as they rounded the corner on to Pulteney Street.

Catherine wanted to tell him that she didn't like John at all, but she decided not to upset her dear brother.

'He seems nice,' she replied.

'And the rest of the family?'

'I like Isabella very much,' Catherine said. 'Very much indeed.'

James agreed, and even Catherine noticed how happy he was to be talking about the pretty girl.

'She is quite the marvel.' He smiled. 'So smart and admired. I'm glad you're spending lots of time with her . . . and I shall too . . .'

CHAPTER EIGHT

After a cheerful lunch with James and Mr and Mrs Allen, Catherine excused herself and spent the afternoon poring over the pages of *Udolpho*.

Who could not find this thrilling? she wondered to herself. It took every scrap of effort she had to tear herself away from the heart-stopping adventure and get ready for the ball when the time came. It felt very wrong to be giving up the wonders of *Udolpho* for the blandness of John Thorpe, but the tingly thrill of arriving at the ball already engaged to dance kept her interested. 'I'll be the envy of every girl without a partner,' she whispered to herself.

The thrill soon wore off, however, when the Thorpes and Allens arrived at the ball and . . .

'Right!' John barked, barely giving Catherine a glance. 'I'm off.' And with that, he clomped straight off to the card room, leaving Catherine feeling angry and completely without a partner.

'ABSOLUTELY NOT!' Isabella protested too loudly when James asked her if she would dance with him. She flailed her arms and gasped dramatically. 'There is no way I'm taking a single step on to the floor until John is back and Catherine can join us. I just COULDN'T leave her alone with no one to dance with, and she'll NEVER find us in the crowd later on!'

Catherine smiled at this and was grateful that her friend wanted to stay with her while John had abandoned them, but the moment James had turned his back, Isabella leant over and whispered in Catherine's ear.

'My dear creature, I'm afraid I must leave you. Your brother won't stop protesting and is dreadfully impatient to dance . . .'

Catherine hadn't noticed James protesting at all, but she smiled and nodded.

'I knew you wouldn't mind,' Isabella said, squeezing Catherine's hand. 'I'm sure John will be back soon, and you can easily find us in the crowd later.'

Catherine groaned to herself. How could John be so selfish and annoying? All the excitement had turned into nothing, and now she was stuck between Mrs Allen (who only talked about her dresses) and Mrs Thorpe (who only talked about her children) and it was extremely dull.

But . . . all heroines need the occasional plot twist to speed them on the road to adventure, my dear reader, and Catherine was about to experience one in her own story. Sighing to herself, she looked up and there, entering the Bath Assembly Rooms, was . . . Henry Tilney.

Catherine gasped and instantly felt her cheeks flush red.

After all this time, Mr Tilney was walking in her direction, a young woman holding on to his arm. She peered at the beautiful girl with strings of pearls in her hair and Catherine realised that this must be his sister. She remembered he'd mentioned her at their first meeting.

In just a few more steps they'd be passing right next to Mrs Allen and Mrs Thorpe, and Henry was sure to see Catherine sitting between them. Her heart started to pound against the inside of her ribcage like it was trying to play a tune.

'Miss Morland!'

Catherine turned, pretending to only notice Henry and his sister at that moment.

'How wonderful to see you,' he said as a wide smile spread across his face. It was a smile that made Catherine want to turn pale and faint like one of the damsels in *The Mysteries of Udolpho*.

The next few minutes saw Mr Tilney chatting warmly with Mrs Thorpe and Mrs Allen. He explained that he'd left Bath for a week but was now back with his sister, Eleanor.

'Do sit down with us,' Mrs Allen cooed and fussed, thrilled to have another friend at the ball, but Mr Tilney did not sit. Instead, he offered Catherine his hand and asked her to dance.

'I . . . umm . . . well, I . . . you see . . .' Catherine's head was swirling with stress and panic. She desperately wanted to say yes, but there were strict rules at the Bath Assembly Rooms balls and she would cause a scandal if she agreed to dance with Henry when she already had John as a partner.

With a heavy heart, Catherine politely declined Mr Tilney's request and he calmly accepted. Inside her head, she was about to reel off a whole list of insults for John Thorpe, when the squat and plain man appeared, swaggering back from the card room.

'Time to dance!' he exclaimed, taking Catherine by the arm and whisking her away from Henry and his sister without a second's thought.

Catherine was secretly furious. John showed no concern that he'd left her waiting on her own for nearly half an hour. He started to natter and boast about his impressive friends and their hunting dogs, leaving Catherine to gaze miserably at Henry Tilney every time she caught a glimpse of him through the throng of merrymakers.

After two dances were finally over, Isabella and James came bustling through the crowd.

'My dear creature, there you are. I've been searching for you all evening.'

'Isabella!' Catherine whispered, pulling her friend aside. 'Look there.' She pointed as Henry's sister, Eleanor, glided past with a partner of her own. She was beautiful and serene and didn't seem to be interested in the attention of everyone who passed her, in the way that Isabella was.

'That is Miss Tilney,' Catherine continued. 'Henry's sister!'

'Heavens!' Isabella cried with glee. 'Does that mean he is here too? Point him out. I'm dying to see him!'

Catherine searched the crowd for Mr Tilney, but by the time she turned back to her friend, Isabella was teasing James about whether she'd dance with him again and didn't seem particularly interested at all.

'Another dance?' John guffawed, reaching for Catherine's hand.

'No,' she replied a little too quickly, snatching her arm away. 'I . . . umm . . . I'm tired.'

'Let's take a walk then,' he said. 'We can go and make fun of my ugly sisters and their foolish partners.'

Catherine shook her head again, and before anyone could stop her, she hurried off in the direction of Mrs Allen and Mrs Thorpe. When John had dragged her away, Henry had been chatting to the women. Maybe he'd still be with them? Now that Catherine had fulfilled her two dances with John, she was free to find a new partner, and . . .

He was gone.

Catherine could see before she'd even reached the other side of the room.

'Mr Tilney?' Mrs Allen repeated after Catherine had asked after him. 'He was just here moments ago. He said he was tired of lounging about and wanted to dance instead.'

Catherine jolted with happiness. Maybe Henry was looking for her too? She eagerly turned back to the dancers just in time to see him walking on to the floor with . . . with a pretty young lady he'd met elsewhere in the room.

'Ah, he has got a partner,' Mrs Allen sighed. 'I wish he'd asked you.'

CHAPTER NINE

For the rest of the night, Catherine could hardly hide her unhappiness.

It started as a general irritation of everyone around her at the ball, then grew into a burning desire to get as far away from the Bath Assembly Rooms as she could and go straight home.

When she finally reached Pulteney Street with Mr and Mrs Allen, Catherine went to the pantry and snacked on any tidbits of food she could find. It wasn't because she was hungry exactly but because it distracted her from her misery.

Next, she found herself slumping into bed and without bothering to brush her hair or fold her clothes from that evening, she fell into a deep sleep and didn't wake for nine hours.

By the time she woke the following morning, Catherine's glumness had thankfully trickled away, and she climbed out of bed feeling much calmer and clearer of mind.

'I shall go to the Grand Pump Room and properly get to know Eleanor Tilney,' she thought out loud to herself as she finally combed last night's knots out of her hair. 'Someone who has just arrived in Bath is sure to be there at lunchtime to meet old acquaintances and make new ones.'

With that, Catherine formulated a plan to spend the morning reading *Udolpho* in the peace of her bedroom, and then she'd dress as beautifully as she could and head to the tea rooms for one o'clock. If Eleanor was there, and she definitely had to be, it would give Catherine the perfect chance to make friends with her. That way she'd also get to know Henry better.

Her idea was foolproof . . . or so she thought . . .

'Miss Morland!'

The voice bellowed from some other part of the lodgings, making Catherine jump and drop her novel on to the floor. She hurried to her door, opened it, and found John Thorpe was halfway up the staircase, hollering and yelling.

'Catherine, here I am!' he barked when he saw her. 'Have you been waiting impatiently for me?'

'Waiting for what?'

'Oh, come now, have you forgotten our engagement?' John said, frowning. 'We agreed to take a ride together.'

'I remember something about it, but I wasn't expecting you today.' Catherine practically winced. What about her plans to see Eleanor Tilney?

'Hurry, Miss Morland. James and Isabella are waiting too.'

Catherine's hopes immediately brightened. If her brother and Isabella were coming along for the ride as well, it couldn't be too bad. Miss Tilney would have to wait until tomorrow.

'Quick, now!' John ordered, making Catherine run back into her bedroom and dress as quickly as she could.

Ten minutes later she emerged on to Pulteney Street to see John sitting alone on his carriage, while Isabella and James were in their own one behind.

'My dearest creature, we've been waiting for THREE HOURS!' Isabella moaned when she spotted her friend stepping outside. 'Wasn't last night's ball wonderful?'

Catherine didn't have an answer to Isabella's

question and she certainly didn't want to lie so she smiled, took John's hand and climbed into the seat next to him.

'He's full of spirits,' John said, nodding to his horse. 'Don't be afraid if he dances about a bit. He's skittish and playful as can be but will soon know his master.'

Catherine didn't exactly like the sound of an overexcited horse and she was feeling a little disheartened by the unexpected twist in the morning's plans but resigned herself to sit back and enjoy the ride.

'Let's go!' John yelled.

In no time the two carriages were speeding out of town, coursing up and down countryside lanes and splashing through shallow streams. Catherine found the sunlight on her face and the breeze through her hair actually quite lovely. The morning outing would have been almost perfect if she wasn't stuck with John Thorpe for the entire time.

The man was a complete bore! They hadn't

even passed the Grand Pump Room before he was boasting about all kinds of nonsense that Catherine couldn't care less about.

She closed her eyes and tried to block out his voice as he droned on and on, telling her of horses he'd bought for pennies and sold for a fortune, racing matches he'd predicted the winners for, how he'd shot hundreds of birds and expertly guided his pack of hounds on hunts.

After a while, Catherine began to question the sanity of her dear friend and brother. How could they both like John so much when he was clearly what Mrs Allen would describe as 'most disagreeable'?

When they returned to Pulteney Street again that afternoon, Catherine almost burst out laughing when she overheard Isabella remarking that she 'couldn't believe it was three o'clock already'. According to her friend, time spent with James in the second carriage had been so wonderfully amusing, it felt like they'd only been out a tiny while.

Catherine would never admit it to anyone, but her time spent with John felt like it had gone on for a week. She lovingly bade farewell to Isabella and James and headed inside for a moment's quiet.

Quiet didn't exactly come, though . . .

No sooner had Catherine closed the front door to the street, Mrs Allen wobbled down the staircase in her direction, wanting to talk all about the afternoon she'd had.

To make matters even worse, it turned out that her dress-obsessed chaperone had spent all of lunch at the Grand Pump Room and walking along the Royal Crescent with none other than Henry and Eleanor Tilney.

Catherine didn't scream at that moment like one of the horrified maidens in *The Mysteries of Udolpho*, but she certainly wanted to.

CHAPTER TEN

The next few days passed by without very much happiness in them. Catherine met Isabella and James at the theatre in the evening after their ride through the countryside, but the pair were so interested in each other, they almost failed to notice Catherine was even there.

She did finally manage to fulfil her ambition of seeing Eleanor at the Grand Pump Room, which was a real spot of luck, especially after she worried herself half-sick that John Thorpe would ruin her plans again.

Conversation with Miss Tilney was polite and friendly, but she had arrived at the meeting hall with a Mrs Hughes who kept fussing in and out of their talk and interrupting them.

Apart from some kind chatter and the definite feeling that they would grow into stronger friends, Catherine's only joy was finding out that the Tilneys (including Henry and Eleanor's father, General Tilney) would be at the country dance the following night.

This was her chance to see Henry and partner herself with him again. The thought of it made her skin prickle with goosebumps.

So . . . when the time came to prepare herself for the ball, she dressed in the finest gown she owned and made her way to the Bath Assembly Rooms with Mr and Mrs Allen.

The ball was heaving and very crowded when they arrived, but no matter where she turned, Catherine couldn't seem to get away from John Thorpe. Everywhere she stepped, he was there, smiling and snorting and saying something brainless.

In the tiniest amount of time, John had begun to repel poor Catherine. His comments and his constant talk about dogs, horses and his idiotic carriage made her skin crawl. If dear Isabella hadn't been his sister, she would have gladly never spoken to the dull man again.

Even worse was the constant fear that John was going to ask her to dance! There was no way she could allow herself to be promised to another partner before Henry arrived, so Catherine decided to pretend she couldn't hear John over the music every time he spoke to her.

There were a few awkward moments when Catherine had to practically hide from Isabella's brother, but finally . . . FINALLY!!! . . . Mr Tilney appeared through the crowd and asked her to dance.

'Wait a minute,' John blurted over Catherine's

shoulder as she took Henry's arm. 'Who's he? I thought you were engaged to me for the evening, no?'

Catherine ignored him.

'What's the meaning of this? You're my partner!'

'I don't know why you'd think so,' Catherine said flatly to the red-faced John. 'You did not ask me.'

'By Jove!' John scoffed. 'By heavens!'

Catherine half expected to see steam coming out of his ears, but before he could stop himself, John had a complete change of mind and started asking Henry if he wanted to buy a horse from him. His irritated ranting then dwindled to nothing but mumbling as a line of beautiful young women paraded past, and with that, John was gone . . . snuffling like a blockheaded basset hound after rabbits.

'If he had stayed here even a minute longer,'

Henry said with a mischievous grin, leading Catherine on to the floor, 'I think I would have lost my patience and taken a nap right here among the dancers.'

Catherine spent the evening in a daze of excited glee. She couldn't believe her luck that Mr Tilney had asked her to be his partner after she'd declined his offer at the last ball. Now that they were twirling around, she didn't think she'd ever been happier to be in Bath.

They joked and laughed with one another as the music played louder and louder, and Henry teased Catherine about her life in a country village and her *fascinating* conversations with Mrs Allen.

Catherine knew she shouldn't, but she couldn't help but laugh, and it made Henry visibly happy when she did.

***

The only moment when a sense of unease crept around the two young revellers was when a tall, handsome gentleman approached them both and whispered something in Henry's ear, before marching away proudly through the crowd.

Catherine, worrying that he was someone coming to warn Henry she wasn't well-to-do or pretty enough, turned her head away in embarrassment.

'Don't worry.' Henry smiled when he saw Catherine's discomfort. 'That, Miss Morland, was my father.'

'General Tilney!' she gasped.

'It seems he knows your name already, so there's no reason you shouldn't know his.'

'I would like to meet him properly one day,' Catherine said, feeling a little nervous. The grand gentleman looked very stern and not altogether friendly.

'You shall,' Henry promised. 'But before then, I'd like to invite you for a country walk with my sister, Eleanor.'

Catherine's heart jumped up into her throat.

'Oh, yes!' She beamed.

'Eleanor mentioned you both chatted at the Grand Pump Room and I know she'd love to get to know you better.'

'As would I,' Catherine replied, grinning with wide eyes. 'Let's do it as soon as possible. TOMORROW!'

'Perfect,' said Henry. 'When shall we call to collect you?'

'Twelve o'clock,' Catherine said. 'So long as the weather is good. I'm certain it will be.'

'Perfect,' Henry said again with a smile.

And with that, the music drew to a close and the ball began to empty. Catherine had searched for Isabella before leaving, but her friend was nowhere to be seen. She didn't really mind. The dancing may have been over for the evening, but as Catherine walked home with Mr and Mrs Allen, she still danced about like an excited toddler inside her swirling head.

CHAPTER ELEVEN

The following morning, Catherine practically leapt out of bed. She ran straight to the window and threw open the heavy drapes.

'Oh, no!' she wailed, feeling a surge of disappointment wash over her.

The view that spread out before her was that of a very grey and dreary-looking Pulteney Street. The sky was thick with clouds and Catherine even spotted one or two umbrellas being carried by passers-by.

'How I hate the sight of an umbrella,' she said to herself. 'No walk for me today . . . but, perhaps it will brighten before twelve.'

Deciding it was far too early to give up hope of seeing Henry and Eleanor later, Catherine dressed quickly and went down to the drawing room where she could watch the weather far more comfortably.

'I have no doubt in the world it's going to be a fine day,' Mrs Allen comforted her guest absentmindedly, but when raindrops started pitter-patting on the windows at eleven o'clock, she changed her mind. 'Oh! Dear, I believe it will be wet.'

Catherine didn't know what to do. Every five minutes she would run to the clock, then rush back to glance out the window.

'It's hopeless,' she sighed when twelve o'clock arrived and it was now heavily raining. 'The Tilneys won't venture out in this.'

'You will not be able to go, my dear, as I warned you,' said Mrs Allen, her mind wandering as usual. 'Such a pity. I knew it would rain.'

But, by the time half past twelve arrived, the clouds miraculously started to clear, and the sun brightened the grey sky. There were even patches of blue peeking through.

'I always knew it would clear up.' Mrs Allen nodded, failing to notice Catherine rolling her eyes.

All at once the place was bustling with activity. Mr Allen quickly decided he would venture off to the Grand Pump Room, but Mrs Allen, after trotting back and forth to her rooms with various hats and shawls, decided the streets would be far too dirty to join him.

Catherine was just waving Mr Allen off from the front door when she spotted the same two open carriages, containing the same three people who had surprised her with a ride a few mornings back.

'Isabella, my brother and Mr Thorpe!' she gasped to Mrs Allen. 'They're coming for me, but I will not go.'

In moments, John Thorpe was at the door demanding that Catherine 'Make haste!'.

'Put on your hat this instant. There's no time to waste!' he barked up the stairs.

'But Mr Thorpe,' Catherine called frantically, 'I cannot go out with you today. I'm expecting friends any moment now.'

'Friends?' John grunted.

'Yes. Miss Tilney and her brother,' said Catherine. 'They were due to take me on a country walk at twelve, only it rained. Now it's sunny, I'm sure they will be here soon.'

'Tilney?' blurted John. He took Catherine by the arm and led her out on to the pavement where James and Isabella were waiting. 'That fellow you danced with last night? No! You won't see him. Not a chance!'

'Why do you say that?'

'Because,' John sneered, 'as we were riding here to collect you just now, I saw Mr Tilney and a smartly dressed woman riding out of town.'

'It can't be true,' Catherine said, feeling a little saddened. 'That must have been Eleanor.'

'It's completely true. They were turning along the Lansdown Road. They'll be miles outside Bath by now.'

'Oh,' Catherine mumbled. For a second she thought she might even cry. 'I suppose it would be too dirty for a walk.'

'Of course,' John continued. 'It's filthy out. The rain has turned the city into a swamp!'

'My dear creature,' Isabella called over her brother's shoulder. 'You must come out with us today. We're going to visit Blaise Castle!'

Catherine jolted as a tingle of excitement crept down her spine.

'What's that?' she asked.

'It's the oldest castle in the kingdom,' Isabella chuckled with glee. 'There are towers and long galleries by the dozen. It will be just like *Udolpho*!'

'Well . . .' Catherine glanced down the length of Pulteney Street and saw no sign of Henry or Eleanor. She supposed that John might be correct, even though she didn't want him to be. 'All right . . .'

'Splendid!' Isabella cooed.

Catherine was extremely muddled as she clambered into the carriage next to John. She couldn't help but feel a little hurt by Henry and Eleanor. How could they ride out of town without sending so much as a note? But she was now tingling with the promise of seeing a real life castle. The ups and downs of it all made her feel very unsettled.

They were quickly away, coursing down the boulevards. John talked to his horse and Catherine's thoughts raced between beautiful sights and broken promises, castle dungeons and Henry's smile, trap doors and spoiled plans.

It wasn't until they were riding down Argyle

Buildings, however, that John spoke to her and shook Catherine from her daydreaming.

'Who is that girl who was staring at you so harshly?' he asked.

'Who? Where?'

'On the pavement, just there,' John replied.

Catherine twisted in her seat and saw Eleanor Tilney leaning on Henry's arm, walking slowly down the street. They were both glancing back at her with a look of confusion on their faces.

'Stop! Stop, Mr Thorpe!' Catherine cried. 'It's Henry and Eleanor Tilney!'

As if in answer to her surprise, John let out a snicker and pushed his horse into a faster trot, racing round the next corner.

'How could you tell me they were gone?' Catherine snapped at him. 'Stop! I must go back to Miss Tilney.' But John only laughed more and rode on harder.

Catherine had never felt so angry in her life.

'How could you lie to me? Why did you say you saw the Tilneys leaving town? They must think I'm so rude. You cannot possibly know how vexed I am, Mr Thorpe. You lied! YOU LIED!'

John just shrugged. 'It must have been someone

else who looked just like them,' he said with a vinegary smile.

'I'll never enjoy myself now,' Catherine sobbed. 'Today is ruined.'

And . . . Catherine wasn't wrong, my dear reader. The day was indeed spoiled, and nothing could cheer up Miss Morland as they wound their way along country roads.

To make matters worse, the party of castle-hunters didn't even reach their destination. After more than an hour of riding, James called out from the second carriage.

'John! We left too late!' he yelled. 'This journey is far longer than we'd imagined. Your sister agrees. We should turn back before we're stuck out here in the dark.'

'It must be put off until another day,' Isabella joined in.

'Ugh!' John grunted, yanking on his horse's

reigns. He'd fallen into a bad mood. 'I couldn't care either way.'

They spent the evening in the Thorpes' lodgings in Edgar Buildings. Catherine was upset and couldn't raise her spirits, but Isabella didn't seem to take it seriously.

'Don't be so grumpy,' she playfully whispered to Catherine between a round of cards. 'You will break my heart!'

Catherine didn't reply. Why wasn't her friend showing any sign of sympathy after what had happened? Isabella knew how much she wanted to spend more time with Henry.

'I blame all today's nonsense on the Tilneys. My brother was completely innocent,' Isabella said, not looking up. 'Henry and his sister should have been more punctual. This is all their fault.'

And now, my dear reader, it's time to leave

Catherine for a little while. Our heroine did not get any happier that evening and fell asleep on a pillow wet with tears.

Let's leave the poor thing in peace for a while and skip ahead to the next day. Things will be brighter then, I'm sure . . .

CHAPTER TWELVE

'Mrs Allen,' Catherine said as she came into the drawing room the following morning. 'Would you mind if I visit Miss Tilney today? I feel so uncomfortable and won't be right until I explain everything that happened yesterday.'

'Wear a white dress, dear,' was Mrs Allen's reply. 'Miss Tilney always wears white.'

In her best white dress, Catherine made her way towards Milsom Street where General Tilney had his lodgings. She rushed as fast as she could, keeping her eyes low to avoid seeing Isabella and her family, who she knew were in a shop nearby.

When she reached the correct address, or at least the address that Mrs Allen had told her, Catherine knocked and prayed she'd come to the right place.

'May I speak to Miss Tilney?' she asked when a servant came to the door.

The man told her that he didn't know if Eleanor was at home and asked her name.

'Catherine Morland. I so wish to speak to Eleanor urgently.'

The servant went back inside, then a few minutes later he reappeared and told Catherine that Miss Tilney was not at home and she could not see her.

Catherine's heart sank. Something told her that Eleanor was indeed at home but had refused to come to the door. She walked away slowly, daring to glance up at the drawing room windows to see if Miss Tilney was there, looking down at her.

She wasn't . . .

But, at the bottom of the street, Catherine turned back again and gasped when she spotted

Eleanor stepping out from the front door of their home with General Tilney.

'It's all ruined,' Catherine whimpered to herself and she ran back to Pulteney Street feeling completely mortified.

Dejected and humbled, Catherine didn't want to go to the theatre that evening with Mr and Mrs Allen, but she couldn't think of a good enough excuse to stay home, and in her misery, the idea of watching a new play pricked at her curiosity.

As they took their seats, she was relieved to see that none of the Tilneys had come out for the evening, and after four acts of the comedy that rumbled about the stage, she started to relax and even enjoy herself.

It was just as the fifth and final act of the night was beginning, however, that movement on the other side of the theatre caught Catherine's attention and she looked across to see Henry and General Tilney entering the balcony.

Suddenly, all the anxiety and stress she'd been feeling throughout the day rushed back and Catherine could barely listen to the actors on stage. Every other look was directed straight across the dark auditorium and eventually, just when she thought she'd never catch his eye, Henry glanced across at her, stared for a moment without smiling, bowed his head and turned back to the play.

The curtain fell . . . The lights came up and . . . and . . . Henry wasn't in his seat! Catherine glanced about the theatre but couldn't see him anywhere. She made a dash to exit into the foyer, deciding that she simply *had* to explain herself, burst through the door and ran straight into Mr Tilney himself. He'd come around to see her!

Henry opened his mouth to speak, but Catherine was far beyond being polite and waiting her turn.

'Oh! Mr Tilney, I've been quite wild to speak with you and tell you how sorry I am. You must have thought I was so rude, but I promise it was not my fault. Mr Thorpe told me that you and Eleanor had left Bath and so I agreed to go with them on a day trip, but I would much rather have been with you a million times over.'

The corner of Henry's mouth curled into a smile.

'I begged Mr Thorpe to stop the carriage, I

really did!' Catherine went on.

'We were just a little confused,' Henry replied. 'But now you have explained it, I cannot be angry with you.'

'But Eleanor is angry.'

'No,' said Henry.

'She is. Today I called at your house and she had me turned away, but I saw that Eleanor was home. She left the house shortly after me.'

'Ah!' Henry chuckled. 'I heard about that. The truth is, Miss Morland, that Eleanor very much wanted to see you, but my father was just about to set off with her and he *hates* having his plans interrupted by visitors. He refused to allow anybody in, that's all.'

Catherine nearly twirled on the spot; she was so delighted to hear this.

'We must make plans for a new walk,' he said. 'There is no harm done, Miss Morland.'

When the time arrived for the theatre to start

emptying and they parted ways, Catherine was practically the happiest creature in the world. The only thing that distracted from her feeling of total joy was the sight of John Thorpe talking with General Tilney in the theatre lobby. From the way they both muttered quietly and occasionally looked over at her, Catherine could tell that she was the subject of their conversation.

'Oh, no,' Catherine mumbled to herself.

The General had already denied her at his own front door. What if he didn't like the look of her? What if he didn't want Catherine to see his son and daughter?

Her worried questions were finally answered when John Thorpe eventually sidled over to the group and Catherine couldn't stop herself from asking how he knew General Tilney as she'd seen them talking.

'Known him for years,' John boasted. 'I met him at the Bedford Club long ago. We play billiards together. I always beat him!'

Catherine nodded, secretly wishing she could scream at the squat brute standing before her.

'But, what do you think we were talking about?' John teased. 'You! Yes, by heavens. And the General thinks you're the finest girl in Bath!'

'Me!' Catherine was shocked. 'How can you say so?'

'It's true. I told him I think he's absolutely right.' John waggled his eyebrows and Catherine guessed that he was trying to flirt with her.

He continued trying to flatter and woo her while they waited to leave, but Catherine had blocked John out and was completely ignoring him by the time Mr Allen called her away.

General Tilney didn't dislike her, he admired her!

Catherine practically floated the whole way home. The evening had gone so much better than she could have wished for.

CHAPTER THIRTEEN

Sunday arrived, and with it, Isabella, John and James came to Pulteney Street. They had collected Catherine and were taking a stroll through town with the idea of chatting and making plans for a second attempt at reaching Blaise Castle on Monday.

'What?' Isabella gasped.

'I'm very sorry, but I cannot go tomorrow,' said Catherine, looking grave.

'But you must come! We will not go without you. How can you choose a silly walk in the countryside with strangers over me, your best friend?'

'Do not urge me, Isabella. I am engaged with Miss Tilney for the morning. You know this and I cannot go.' Catherine felt extremely distressed but also very resolute.

'Just tell them that you have a prior engagement and you can go the next day instead. Go on Tuesday,' replied Isabella. 'It's easy.'

'No, it is not easy. I could not lie to them,' Catherine said, feeling more and more worried. 'There is no prior engagement.'

Isabella smiled sweetly and spoke as softly as she possibly could.

'But you're my dearest, sweetest friend,' she said. 'How could you refuse someone who loves you as much as I do?'

Catherine shook her head and Isabella wrinkled her nose, suddenly looking like a child about to have a tantrum.

'I cannot help but be jealous,' she wailed, trying a new tactic. 'I have been cast aside for the attention of strangers. I, who loves you so strongly. The Tilneys have taken over everything!'

Catherine felt wounded by how spiteful her friend was being. She often seemed like she cared about nothing but herself. Isabella had already proved that she could be selfish, ungenerous and extremely rude when the time suited her.

Catherine thought all these things, but she said none of them.

'I shall think you very unkind if you refuse, little sister,' James joined in. He put a protective arm round Isabella.

This was the first time her brother had ever said something so openly against Catherine and it filled her with anxiety.

'Why can't we put our trip to the castle off for an extra day?' Catherine reasoned, trying to fix the problem. 'That way everyone can go.' But her idea was only met with groans and 'Absolutely not!' as

John turned on his heel and walked off down the street.

'Please, dearest,' said Isabella, linking her arm through Catherine's.

'I didn't think you were so stubborn,' James scoffed.

'I'm not,' Catherine shot back in desperation. 'But I cannot go. I wish I could please you all, but I will not let the Tilneys down again.'

'I suspect,' Isabella hissed in a low voice, 'she doesn't care at all.'

Catherine felt a pang of anger. Yanking her arm away from Isabella's, she refused to speak another word, leaving the three of them to stand in awkward silence for the next ten minutes until John Thorpe skipped back towards them with a happy look on his face.

'I have settled the matter, and now we may all go tomorrow.' He beamed.

'What do you mean?' Catherine asked.

'I have seen Miss Tilney and made your excuses.'

'You have not!' cried Catherine.

'I have,' John laughed, looking very proud of himself. 'Caught up with Miss Tilney and her brother near the Grand Pump Room and told them you've just remembered a prior engagement. I said you can walk on Tuesday instead, and they said it was fine. So, that's all sorted.'

'Wonderful,' Isabella chimed in. She was suddenly all smiles and good nature again. 'Now we can have our day out as planned.'

'This will not do!' Catherine said. 'I'll have to chase after Eleanor and tell her the truth immediately.' She turned to go but Isabella caught her by the wrist.

'Everything is sorted now,' James yelled at his little sister. 'This is quite ridiculous!'

'I don't care!' Catherine said furiously. 'Mr Thorpe had no right to lie to her. Isabella, LET ME GO!'

'It's no use.' John smirked at her. 'I caught them on the corner of Brock Street. They'll be home by now.'

'Then I will run there immediately!'

With that Catherine broke away from her friend's grasp and she hurried off towards the Tilneys' lodgings.

She darted between shoppers and weaved through the crowd, somehow managing to arrive on Milsom Street so fast that she rounded the corner in time to see Eleanor and Henry walking into their house.

Catherine quickly knocked as she reached the front step and was so desperate to speak to her new friends that she barged straight past the servant when he opened the door.

'I need to speak with the Tilneys,' she cried over her shoulder as she thundered up the stairs.

There was a door directly in front of her when she reached the upstairs landing and Catherine blundered straight through it, only to be stopped in her tracks as she was met by the surprised gaze of General Tilney, Henry and Eleanor.

'I have come in a great hurry. It was a mistake!' The words poured out of her in one enormous jumble. 'I had no prior engagement. John Thorpe lied again. I so want to come on a walk with you. I ran as fast as I could to explain it to you. Please don't think badly of me . . . I refused to wait for the servant . . .'

'That is very good to hear,' Miss Tilney said. 'I am completely convinced you do indeed want to come on our country walk, my dear.'

Catherine looked from one slightly startled face to another, then burst out laughing at how strange her entrance into the Tilney drawing room must have seemed.

'I do apologise,' she giggled. 'I couldn't wait another second to tell you.'

For the rest of the late morning, Catherine sat and drank tea with her new friends. Henry introduced her to General Tilney, who was as polite and charming as she could have wished for. He kindly invited Catherine to join them for dinner one night of the week when Mr and Mrs Allen could spare her, and when the time arrived that she should be setting off for Pulteney Street, the handsome older gentleman escorted her down the staircase to the door, complimenting her every step of the way.

Once she was safely home, Catherine's mind had turned back to Isabella and James. She hated the thought of upsetting her brother and her friend but felt certain that she had made the correct choice.

'You have no doubt done the right thing,' Mr Allen grumbled over dinner, when Catherine explained the day's antics. 'Good people never break promises, and I don't want you going sightseeing with the Thorpes any more. That boy is a fool if ever I saw one, and Isabella is old enough to know better than gallivanting about the countryside in open-top carriages.'

Catherine felt guilty and worried for her dear friend, but Mr Allen's words calmed and soothed her. It was certain that everything had turned out just as it should.

CHAPTER FOURTEEN

The next morning was bright and fair and although Catherine was dreading another attack from James, John and Isabella, having Mr Allen close by steadied her nerves.

The Tilneys arrived at the decided time and without any trouble from the Blaise Castle party, and Catherine set off with Eleanor and Henry to walk around Beechen Cliff.

'It reminds me of the South of France,' Catherine sighed as she took in the beautiful view and breathed the clean air.

'A-ha!' Henry cheered. 'I didn't know you'd travelled abroad, Miss Morland.'

'Oh! I haven't,' Catherine said, blushing. 'I only know from what I've read in books. It reminds me of the country in the *The Mysteries of Udolpho* . . . but you never read novels, I'm sure?'

'Why not?'

'Because they are silly and not clever enough for you. I heard that gentlemen read better books.'

'Anyone who doesn't enjoy a good novel must be very stupid indeed!' Henry said with mischief in his eyes. 'I couldn't put *The Mysteries of Udolpho* down. From the moment I opened the book I was gripped, and my hair stood on end for two days!'

'I remember,' Eleanor joined in. 'You refused to let me finish it before you.'

'I'll never be ashamed of reading *Udolpho* again,' Catherine laughed. 'I'm amazed. I was told that men despise novels.'

'Only the stupid ones . . .'

Catherine tingled with glee to learn that Henry loved novels, and she was even more delighted that he'd confirmed John Thorpe was indeed stupid.

The rest of the walk breezed by in a happy jumble of laughter and admiration. Henry and

Eleanor talked about all kinds of things from history and art, to poetry and politics. She was impressed at how funny and silly and brilliantly educated they both were and by how much they knew about the world.

It wasn't until the three of them arrived back on Pulteney Street that Catherine realised she'd not thought about Isabella or James once.

As Mrs Allen welcomed her guests back inside, Eleanor greeted the fussing woman and asked for her permission to have Catherine's company for dinner on Wednesday night.

Mrs Allen agreed at once, and Catherine was happier than she ever thought she could be.

CHAPTER FIFTEEN

Early the next day, a note arrived from Isabella. It was filled with so much kindness and love that it seemed like she'd completely forgotten about their argument on Sunday.

The note begged Catherine to hurry over to the Thorpes' lodgings in Edgar Buildings to hear some wonderful news. She quickly dressed and set off, feeling lighter and more enthusiastic about seeing her friend than she had for the past two days.

When she arrived, Catherine found Isabella's younger sisters, Anne and Maria, in the parlour. When Anne was sent off to fetch Isabella, Maria told Catherine all about how she'd gone on the day trip to Blaise Castle in her place, but that they hadn't reached the old building at all. In fact, it sounded like they hadn't even bothered trying to get anywhere close. Plus, it had rained, and they nearly didn't make it back after James's horse turned out to be far too old and tired for the journey.

Catherine smiled to herself, knowing that she had definitely made the right decision.

'John would only allow me in the carriage next to him,' Maria said smugly. 'He refused to let Anne in because her ankles are far too thick.'

Shortly, Isabella appeared at the door and sent both Anne and Maria away. She rushed into the room and embraced Catherine with so much joy it looked like she might burst.

'You've already guessed, haven't you?' Isabella cooed.

'I . . . umm . . .' Catherine didn't know what her friend was talking about.

'I knew you would. You've got such a sharp eye. Only you know how happy my heart is. James is just the most wonderful person and I can only wish that I was more worthy of him.'

Catherine had started to catch up with Isabella's ramblings.

'You mean?' she gasped. 'Oh, my dear friend, can you really mean you're in love with James?'

'Not only that!' Isabella cried, clapping her hands. 'He loves me too and we are engaged both in hearts and minds. We are to marry!'

Catherine was speechless. This was delightful news and she instantly forgot all about their quarrel only a couple of days back.

'You mustn't tell a soul,' Isabella giggled as she grabbed Catherine in a hug. 'Your brother is setting off to Fullerton today to seek your parents' permission and, with all luck, we should have their answer by tomorrow. TOMORROW!'

The pair hurried out to the hall where James was preparing to leave for the Morland family home.

Catherine could barely get a word out to her brother between happy sobs. He kissed her on the forehead and ran out into the street as Isabella called behind him, telling him to hurry and be as fast as he could.

Catherine was with Isabella for the whole of the following day, determined to keep her spirits up while she waited to hear back from James. As the morning began, Isabella was full of glee and confidence, but by the time the note arrived with James's reply inside, she'd worked herself into such a nervous state it was amazing that she could stand up straight.

The answer was simple . . .

I have had no difficulty in gaining the consent of my kind parents.

That was it. The Thorpe household was filled with tears and laughter. Isabella danced around the room, while Mrs Thorpe was a bundle of tears and joy.

Catherine looked on happily as her friend celebrated the love of James, and she thought how nice it would be to have them living near Fullerton once they were wed. Life certainly wouldn't be so sleepy and dull if Isabella lived nearby.

'Well, Miss Morland.' A voice spoke behind her, making her jump. 'I have come to say goodbye.'

She turned and saw John standing in the doorway. He sidled over and leered at her with a crooked grin.

'What do you think of all this marrying scheme? I say it's not bad.'

'I think it's wonderful,' Catherine replied.

'Do you now?' John said, waggling his eyebrows again. 'I've heard an old saying that going to weddings makes other ladies want to get married. You are coming to Isabella's special day, aren't you?'

'Yes, of course.'

'Good . . . then we can see if the old saying is really true,' said John, trying to look dashing. 'I shall also come and see you in Fullerton when you have returned.'

'If you wish,' Catherine replied. She wasn't really listening to what the horrible man had to say. 'I know my parents will be glad to meet you.'

'Yes?'

'Certainly,' she said, caring nothing for him and only thinking about her dear friend's wedding and dinner with Eleanor. 'We shall see you in Fullerton whenever is convenient.'

With that Catherine walked away, leaving John entirely convinced he'd won Miss Morland's heart and had nothing but her total encouragement to declare his love.

CHAPTER SIXTEEN

Catherine was so excited to have dinner with the Tilneys that it was almost doomed to never live up to her giddy hopes.

She had hurried across town to Milsom Street, filled with happiness at the thought of getting to know Henry and Eleanor so much better, but by the time she had arrived home a few hours later, her feet dragged heavily with disappointment.

What had gone wrong?

In bed, she replayed the whole event over and over again in her head but just couldn't put her finger on what had happened . . .

General Tilney had greeted Catherine with

great kindness, and Eleanor had been equally welcoming, but her friendly chats and the relaxed feeling of their walk in the countryside had completely vanished, making the entire evening more awkward and silent than she could stand. Eleanor seemed nervous and twitchy, and Henry hardly spoke a word throughout dinner. Catherine had never seen him so quiet and sheepish.

General Tilney couldn't possibly be to blame. He seemed so kind and practically showered her with compliments all the time she was having dinner with his family. Something else must be the cause . . .

'Pride,' said Isabella, pulling a face like she was tasting something sour. 'I've always thought it. They are overflowing with haughtiness and pride!'

'I'm not sure,' Catherine muttered, wondering if it had been a good idea to tell Isabella about yesterday night's strangeness.

'Miss Tilney is more stuck-up and spoiled than

anyone else I've ever met,' Isabella continued. 'Imagine treating your own guest so terribly!'

'It wasn't that bad,' Catherine argued back. 'She just seemed unusually shy . . . Henry too.'

'Don't defend them,' said Isabella. 'Eleanor is hateful, and Henry just isn't worthy of you.'

'Worthy of me?' Catherine gasped. 'I don't suppose he'd ever think of me in . . . that way.'

'Exactly! He doesn't think of you! He's nothing like our wonderful brothers. I truly believe that John has the biggest heart. Not like the Tilneys.'

'You can't say that about General Tilney,' Catherine said, feeling a little vexed. 'He was kind and very welcoming to me.'

'I didn't say anything about him,' Isabella shot back. 'He's a total gentleman. John thinks very highly of General Tilney and we both know that John has superb judgement. It's his children I can't stand.'

'Well,' said Catherine with a glint of hope in her eye, 'we can see how they behave tonight.

Eleanor and Henry are joining us at the Bath Assembly Rooms later.'

Isabella groaned.

'Don't you want to go?' Catherine asked.

'I could never say no to you, sweet creature, but without my darling James here in Bath, I refuse to dance. I won't do it. I will turn down absolutely anybody who asks me. No dancing! Not me! You mustn't try and convince me, Catherine.'

'I won't,' Catherine said with a contented smile.

'Good!'

Isabella's opinion of Henry and Eleanor didn't make Catherine think any less of them. She felt certain that neither were filled with haughtiness and pride and was happily proved correct when they both arrived and were completely lovely to her. Eleanor went to great trouble to make sure she spent lots of time at Catherine's side, while Henry asked her if she would join him for a dance.

Before the musicians began to play and it was time to move on to the floor, however, Catherine noticed a tall and very handsome man who seemed to have become part of their group. After some careful whispering to Eleanor, she discovered that this was their eldest brother, Captain Frederick Tilney.

Catherine examined him quietly. He was certainly an impressive figure, possibly more handsome than Henry but a lot sterner and less likeable. She overheard him complaining to his sister that he hated balls, and he even laughed at Henry for wanting to dance.

Of course, Catherine was very glad that Henry took no notice of his big brother and he was soon leading her around the floor, laughing and chatting as always. She found him wonderful when they danced, listening to every word he had to say with wide, sparkling eyes and a smile on her face.

★★★

At the end of the first dance, Frederick crossed the floor and pulled Henry away, which irritated Catherine greatly. She watched as they went to a corner of the hall to talk in hushed voices, instantly making her worry. The familiar fears that some awful rumour about her was being spread or that Frederick was telling Henry off for dancing with someone so low and commonplace filled her head.

So, you can imagine, my dear reader, how relieved and slightly shocked she was when Henry returned and told Catherine that Frederick wanted to dance with Isabella.

'Oh!' she gasped, turning to study her friend, who was sitting looking bored on the other side of the room. 'I'm very sure Isabella doesn't want to dance at all. She said so earlier.'

Henry returned to his brother and gave him the news, then Frederick pulled a face and walked off through the crowd.

'I'm sure your brother won't mind,' Catherine said when Henry joined her again. 'I heard him say he hated dancing. It was very nice of him to ask after Isabella, though. He must have seen her sitting alone and wondered if she'd like a partner.'

'How sweet you are.' Henry smiled. 'You are so kind that you can only imagine my brother is just as kind as you.'

Catherine blushed and the dancing continued.

It wasn't until she heard Isabella's voice nearby that Catherine looked up and saw her standing a little way off preparing to dance with Frederick.

Isabella spotted that Catherine had seen her, then simply shrugged and smiled.

'I can't believe it,' Catherine said to Henry as they twirled around the floor again. 'She was so determined not to dance.'

'People change their minds,' said Henry.

'I'm just shocked,' Catherine replied. 'Isabella said she could never dance without James here . . . I thought she was very firm about it.'

The two friends didn't have a chance to chat until the musicians finally stopped playing for the evening.

'I can see why you were surprised,' Isabella said when she saw the look on Catherine's face. 'I am tired to death, and all I wanted . . . the whole time . . . was to sit down and rest.'

'Why didn't you then?'

'Oh, my dear! He wouldn't let me, and it would have seemed rude, which you know I hate being. You have no idea how much he begged and pleaded. I told him to pick any other girl in the room, but he said he couldn't bear to think of anybody else. He wanted to be with *me*.'

Catherine wasn't sure she believed her friend's story.

'I saw every eye was upon us,' Isabella chuckled with glee.

'Well, he is very handsome.'

'Handsome?' Isabella asked, pretending she hadn't noticed. She shrugged again. 'I suppose he's all right.'

The next time Catherine saw Isabella, she had called by the Thorpes' lodgings and found they had far more interesting things than Frederick Tilney to talk about.

A second letter had just arrived from James saying that if he and Isabella waited for two and a half years before getting married, Mr Morland would give them an allowance of four hundred pounds a year so they could live happily and comfortably together for the rest of their lives.

'Four hundred pounds!' Catherine gasped. 'That's wonderful!' (Don't forget, my dear reader, that back in the days when our heroine's story is taking place, four hundred pounds was a lot of money.)

'It is very charming indeed,' Isabella whimpered with a grave face.

'Mr Morland has been very generous,' Mrs Thorpe said, looking anxiously at her daughter. 'And I'm sure he'll offer you even more in the future. I only wish I could offer so much.'

'I don't want more for myself,' Isabella snapped at her mother. 'I want James to have more. Four hundred pounds is such a small amount to live on . . . but not for me. I never ask for anything.'

'You're so unselfish, my dear,' Mrs Thorpe cooed. 'No one in the world is as loved as you. I dare say that when Mr Morland sees you, he may give you more.'

'We all make horrible mistakes,' Isabella said sourly. 'And everybody has the right to do what they want with their own money . . . even if it's choosing to keep it for themselves.'

Catherine, who had been watching all of this silently, suddenly felt extremely hurt by Isabella's accusations.

'I'm very sure that my father has promised to give as much as he can afford,' she said.

'It's not that, my sweet Catherine,' Isabella corrected herself. 'You both know I'd happily live on far less. I'd be quite content with fifty pounds a year.'

'We know, dear. You are so gracious,' Mrs Thorpe gushed.

Catherine said nothing . . .

'I hate money,' Isabella declared dramatically. 'The thing that really upsets me is the two and a half year wait until *James* gets his money.'

'Yes, yes, my darling Isabella,' said Mrs Thorpe. 'It's perfectly understandable and we can only love you even more for worrying.'

Catherine's feeling of discomfort slowly began to fade away. She started to believe that the long wait was Isabella's main worry, and when she saw her as cheerful and friendly as ever at their next jaunt to the Grand Pump Room, she did her best to forget the unkind things that Isabella had said about her father.

James soon arrived back in Bath and with his warm welcome, all was good again.

CHAPTER SEVENTEEN

The next morning marked six weeks since the Allens had brought Catherine to Bath, and for the past few days she had been listening to their conversations with a beating heart about whether it was time to pack up and return home to Wiltshire. Everything that made her happy seemed at stake.

So, she was completely delighted when Mr Allen announced that they had finally decided to book their lodgings for another two weeks. Nothing could have filled her heart with more happiness, and in her excitement, Catherine rushed across town to visit Eleanor and tell her the good news.

'I'm staying for another fortnight!' she cheered when Eleanor greeted her in the entrance hallway.

There was a strange silence and Eleanor's face fell. It looked like she might burst out crying at any moment.

'What is it?' Catherine asked, suddenly terribly worried that the thought of spending two more weeks with her was bad news for Eleanor.

'Father has decided we are leaving Bath at the end of the week,' Eleanor said with sad, watery eyes.

'The end of the week?'

'We have both tried to persuade him to stay longer, but once he's made up his mind, there's no changing it.'

'I'm so sorry to hear this,' said Catherine dejectedly. 'If I had known before—'

'Perhaps . . .' Eleanor interrupted. 'Well . . . I'd like to ask . . . it would make me very happy if . . .'

General Tilney walked in from the parlour and

Eleanor was instantly silent. He welcomed Catherine with his usual politeness then turned to his daughter and said, ‘Have you done it yet, Eleanor?’

‘I was just about to,’ she answered.

‘Well, carry on by all means, I know how much you wanted to ask Miss Morland.’

‘Ask me what?’ said Catherine.

Eleanor opened her mouth to speak, but General Tilney butted in before she could say anything.

‘My daughter, Miss Morland, has been coming up with a very bold plan. We leave Bath this coming Saturday. You see, I came here to see my friends, the Marquis of Longtown and General Courteney, but sadly they chose not to visit. There is no reason for me to stay in Bath any longer, and Eleanor would like to ask if you’d leave the city with us. Would you quit this lively scene and join us in Gloucestershire at Northanger Abbey?’

NORTHANGER ABBEY! The words were thrilling to Catherine and sent a tingle of anticipation up her spine.

'I have already called in to see Mr and Mrs Allen,' General Tilney continued, 'and they are very happy for you to join us.'

'They are?' Catherine beamed.

'Indeed,' said the General. 'But we will need the permission of your parents, Mr and Mrs Morland, too.'

'I will write home straight away,' Catherine said, fizzing with glee. 'I'm sure they won't object.'

With that, our heroine ran back to Pulteney Street, her mind filled with suspense and a feeling of perfect bliss. She was going to be a guest of the Tilneys! They actually wanted to spend time with her. Eleanor would become her new best friend. Henry would become her . . . she didn't dare to think it.

With Henry at her heart, and Northanger Abbey on her lips, she reached Pulteney Street and dashed to her room to write a note bound for her parents.

'An abbey!' she laughed out loud as she scrawled. 'I'm going to stay in an actual abbey.'

As she wrote, visions of towers and damp passageways, narrow cells and ruined chapels, wailing ghosts and murdered nuns danced through the air around her, and all of it was completely wonderful!

CHAPTER EIGHTEEN

With her thoughts so full of happiness, Catherine had hardly noticed that two or three days had passed without her seeing Isabella. It didn't even cross her mind until she was at the Grand Pump Room one morning with Mrs Allen and discovered she had no one to talk to.

Eventually that day, however, the two girls' paths crossed, and Isabella invited Catherine to sit with her, declaring she had secret news.

'I love this spot,' said Isabella as they sat down on the bench between the two doors leading to the street. 'It's so out of the way.'

Catherine raised one eyebrow questioningly.

Their seat wasn't out of the way at all. With people entering the hall on both sides of them, it seemed busier than any place in the whole building. She watched as Isabella glanced from one door to the next and back again. Who was she searching for?

'Don't worry, Isabella,' Catherine said with a smile. 'James will be here soon.'

'Oh, nonsense, my dear creature,' she replied. 'I'm not stupid enough to need James by my side at every moment of the day. I'd hate for us to always be together. We'd be a laughing stock. Everybody would mock us.'

Isabella hadn't looked at Catherine once. Her eyes were still flicking from side to side, examining who was coming and going from the doorways.

'So, you are going to Northanger Abbey, I hear,' she said without looking at her friend. 'I'm thrilled for you. I've heard it's one of the grandest old places in England. I expect you to write and tell me all about it.'

'I will,' said Catherine. 'I'll do my best to describe every bit of it to you . . . umm . . . Isabella, who are you looking for? Are your sisters coming?'

'I'm not looking for anyone. I have to focus my eyes somewhere,' Isabella snapped, then she softened and smiled. 'I'm just a little absentminded. I believe I'm the most absentminded creature in the world.'

'Didn't you say you had secret news for me?'

'Oh! Yes, I have! I told you my mind was far away. I quite forgot it. Well, the thing is, I have just had a letter from my brother, John. I'm sure you can guess what it's about . . .'

'No,' Catherine said.

'Stop playing games!' Isabella teased. 'You know he is head over heels in love with you.'

'With me!?!'

'Don't pretend you don't know! He told me all about it. Just before he was leaving on his last day here, you gave him the most positive encouragement to come and visit you in Fullerton when you returned to your parents. He said so in the letter.'

Catherine was completely astonished.

'I had no idea he felt that way,' she protested. 'I know he asked me to dance on the first day we met, but that's all.'

Isabella stared blankly and said nothing.

'Please, my friend, you must believe me. I don't think I even saw him before he left Bath.'

'Of course you did! It was the morning I received the letter from James saying your father had said yes. He chatted to you alone. He told me.'

'I don't even remember,' Catherine said in amazement. 'Please tell him straight away that he's made a terrible mistake. I don't ever want to be rude about your brother, Isabella, but if there is a man on my mind . . . John is not him.'

Isabella shrugged.

'I'll admit, after I read his letter, I thought it was

a foolish idea. Neither of you have enough money, and that's all that really matters.'

'So, you forgive me and this strange mistake?' said Catherine, trying to ignore her friend's comment about money. 'I did not mean to fool your brother into thinking I loved him.'

'It's fine,' said Isabella. 'We all change our minds about love.'

'But I didn't change my mind. I never loved him!'

'My dearest Catherine,' Isabella continued without listening to her, 'I would never try and hurry you into marriage. If there's one thing I've learnt, it's do not hurry, or you will certainly live to regret it.'

Isabella gasped.

'Look,' she said in a hushed voice. 'It's Frederick Tilney!'

Catherine looked up and saw him entering the Grand Pump Room.

'Don't worry,' said Isabella, frantically smoothing her dress and checking her hair. 'He'll never see us in this out of the way corner.'

The handsome gentleman instantly saw them and made towards the bench between the doors. He sat down on the far side, completely ignoring Catherine at the other end, and leant in close to Isabella.

'Do you always stare at me?' he whispered with a leer.

'Nonsense! I don't stare or search for you. I am very independent and make my own choices,' came Isabella's reply.

'I wish your heart would make its own choices. Then it would choose me.'

'What do you know about hearts? Men don't have them . . .'

'We have eyes,' Frederick said, 'and you are too beautiful to bear.'

'Then I'll turn my back on you,' Isabella teased and shuffled away from him. 'Is that better?'

'Never,' Frederick sighed. 'I can still see your rosy cheek. It is too much to stand and not nearly enough of you at the same time . . .'

Catherine's jaw nearly clattered across the Grand Pump Room floor. She was stunned by Isabella's behaviour and angry for her brother.

Thinking it would be a good idea to get her

friend away from Frederick, Catherine invited Isabella to walk with her and Mrs Allen, but she immediately protested. Isabella was too tired, and it was apparently boring to parade around the Grand Pump Room. Plus, if she moved, her sisters might not see her.

Feeling terrifically confused and upset, Catherine joined Mrs Allen and left the building altogether.

It seemed to her that Frederick Tilney was falling in love with Isabella, and Isabella was encouraging it.

CHAPTER NINETEEN

Catherine spent the next few days trying desperately not to suspect her friend of betraying James. She couldn't bring herself to confront Isabella about it but watched her very closely and . . . well, my dear reader . . . things didn't look good.

When Isabella was alone with her siblings and family in Edgar Buildings or with Catherine and the Allens in Pulteney Street, she was her usual self, but when they went to the Grand Pump Room or the Bath Assembly Rooms in the evening, she was someone completely different.

She constantly accepted the attention of Frederick Tilney and gave him just as much attention as she did her future husband, smiling and whispering with him! What was going on? What on earth was Isabella up to? It was all beyond Catherine's understanding.

There was no way Isabella could be aware of the pain she was causing James, but she didn't seem to care either way. Anyone could see how much Catherine's poor brother was suffering – he looked miserable and uneasy all the time, and it broke her heart.

She was also extremely worried about Frederick. For him to be behaving the way he was towards Isabella, he must not have known about her engagement.

For a small time, Catherine comforted herself knowing that the Tilneys were leaving Bath and Frederick wouldn't be around to cause problems for her brother, but when she later discovered that he was not coming with them and intended to stay longer in the city, she knew something had to be done.

At this rate, both men could end up with their hearts broken.

After many hours of worrying and thinking, Catherine spoke to Henry . . .

'He knows everything,' Henry said seriously. 'All about Isabella's engagement. I told him so myself.'

'Does he?' Catherine asked. 'Then why does he stay here?'

Henry didn't say anything.

'Please make him leave, Henry. The longer he stays, the worse it will be for everybody. Persuade him!'

'I can't persuade him,' Henry said as gently as he could.

'But does he not know how much pain he is causing my brother?'

'Are you sure this is Frederick's fault?'

'Yes!'

'Is it Frederick's interest in Miss Thorpe that's hurting your brother, or Miss Thorpe's delight in all the attention?'

Catherine blushed and knew Henry was right.

'Isabella is so, so wrong,' she said, 'but she can't know how much this is breaking James's heart, she loves him. They have been in love since they first met.'

'There's a chance she does know,' Henry said sadly. 'And . . .'

'You don't think she loves my brother?' Catherine asked.

Henry paused for a long time. His eyes looked sad yet full of kindness towards Catherine.

'Look,' he said, 'try not to worry. It's true Frederick is staying in Bath, but it may only be for a few days. Very soon he will have to return to being the captain of his regiment, and who will he flirt with then? Isabella will soon forget him.'

Catherine heaved a sigh of relief. Henry knew what he was talking about and she trusted him completely. She blamed herself for getting so worried and swore she would not think about it any more.

Her spirit was also brightened when the Thorpes came to say farewell to Catherine on her last night

in Pulteney Street. James was in a fine mood and Isabella seemed a lot like she used to be. There were moments when she glared at her future husband or snatched her hand away from his, but Catherine remembered Henry's words and decided it was just playful teasing.

She soon relaxed and enjoyed the hugs, tears and promises of tomorrow's departure for Northanger Abbey.

CHAPTER TWENTY

'I'll be so sorry to see you go,' Mrs Allen blubbed as her young friend was preparing to leave Pulteney Street. 'You've been a valuable companion.'

'I promise I'll write,' Catherine reassured her. She was secretly far too excited to think of anything else but Henry and Eleanor and visiting a real abbey like the ones in *Udolpho*. 'Farewell!'

Mr Allen walked Catherine and her cases across town to Milsom Street in time to join General Tilney and his family for breakfast.

'Welcome, welcome, Miss Morland.' The General beamed upon her arrival. 'You're just in time.' And no sooner had the door closed behind

Mr Allen, Catherine found that all her happiness was instantly replaced by a feeling of dread.

What if she disappointed her new hosts? How could she possibly stay with such a well-to-do family and not embarrass herself? In only minutes, Catherine had worked herself into such a panic that if Mr Allen had knocked again, she would have left with him and returned to Pulteney Street immediately.

Thankfully, Eleanor's kindness and Henry's smile soon calmed her nerves, but she was still far from relaxed. The General seemed to fuss around her all the time. He was constantly showering Catherine with compliments, worrying whether she was comfortable or if she had enough to eat, despite being seated in front of the biggest breakfast spread she'd ever seen in her life.

It didn't help the tension when General Tilney yelled at Frederick and made him apologise to Catherine after he came downstairs late, and it was worrying to hear him mutter, 'How glad I shall be when you're all off' to Eleanor as they prepared to leave.

Every part of the morning was stressful. The clock struck ten and General Tilney continuously complained that he wanted to have left by now. The two carriages, an open-roofed one and a larger closed stagecoach, were piled high with trunks and boxes, leaving almost no room for the passengers.

When they eventually got moving, General Tilney and Henry rode in the carriage at the front of the group, while Catherine, Eleanor and her maidservant took the one behind.

There were thirty miles between Bath and Northanger Abbey and Catherine finally started to relax in Eleanor's cheerful company. She felt no sadness as they rolled out of the city and enjoyed the new sights on a road she had never taken before. At last she was enjoying herself and chattered happily with her new friend as they sped along country lanes in the direction of Gloucestershire.

At the halfway mark of the journey, the carriages stopped for two hours to rest the horses and give them food and water, and General Tilney was once again fussing around everyone. He constantly checked on his children and seemed to silence them just by being present. He got angry with the waiters in the tavern, complained about the food and made the two hours seem more like four.

At last, the orders were given for the journey to continue, and much to Catherine's surprise, General Tilney suggested she ride in the front open-roofed carriage with Henry.

'It's a fine day and he's eager for you to see as much of the countryside as possible.'

So, with a shy smile and a nod of her head, Catherine found herself in the seat next to Henry, once again gliding through sunlit roads and feeling very happy indeed.

They talked and joked as he drove, and Henry praised her for joining them.

'I'm so thankful you've come,' he said. 'You're a true friend to Eleanor. She's so often alone at Northanger, and I'm grateful you agreed to stay.'

'How can that be?' Catherine asked. 'Eleanor has you for company, no?'

'The abbey is only a half home for me,' Henry explained. 'I have my own house in Woodston, which is about twenty miles from the abbey. I have to spend a lot of time there at my parsonage.'

'You must be very sorry for that.'

'I'm always sorry to leave Eleanor alone.'

'Yes . . . but besides your love for her, it must be so awful to have to live in an ordinary parsonage after Northanger Abbey has been your home.'

Henry smiled.

'You have formed a very lovely idea of what the abbey is like in your head.'

'Of course!' said Catherine. 'It must be a fine old place – just like in all the books I've read.'

'But are you prepared to face all the horrors

that lurk in dark places like the ones in your books?' Henry teased. 'Is your heart strong enough to cope with sliding bookshelves and trapdoors?'

'Yes!' Catherine cried excitedly. 'I don't think I'll be scared, there are lots of people about, aren't there?'

'There are lots of people in the family's side of the house,' Henry continued in a creepy voice.

'What do you mean?'

'When a new young lady visits Northanger Abbey, we demand she stays far apart from the rest of us. While the Tilneys all sleep sweetly in our end of the house, the poor damsel is led away to a lonely, ruined part of the building by Dorothy, the ancient, toothless housekeeper. Down gloomy passages and up winding staircases to a room that no one has slept in since a distant relative died in its cobweb-covered bed!'

'Oh! Stop it!' Catherine giggled nervously. 'That won't happen to me, I'm sure.'

'Your room is dark and dusty with lots of

shadowed corners. In them you may find a dagger discarded long ago, some dreadful cabinet filled with nightmarish things, or a few drops of blood from another poor guest of the family who was foolish enough to stay.'

'No!' Catherine gasped. She was half scared out of her wits, half enjoying Henry's story very much indeed. Just then it started to rain, but she didn't care in the slightest.

'A great storm will rise up and clatter the stained-glass windows, disturb the curtains and flicker the candles. Then, just as you discover there is a secret door behind a tapestry and you open it, the room is plunged into darkness and you are left to face whatever monster you have just released from behind the wall!'

'Oh, no! Do not say so,' Catherine squealed in horrified delight. She waited a moment. 'Well . . . go on!'

But Henry couldn't keep a straight face for a

second longer. He burst out laughing at Catherine with her wide, amazed eyes and did not finish his story.

'Now is not the time for stories,' he eventually chuckled. 'We are arriving.'

Catherine twisted in her seat and gawped about, looking for signs of towers and turrets above the tree line, but there was nothing.

As they rounded a bend in the road, she saw that Northanger Abbey was a low drab building, not nearly as petrifying as she'd imagined.

In no time, the carriages were under the covered porch and safe from the rain, and Catherine was led into the entrance hall, where the General and Eleanor were already waiting for her.

She would never admit it to any of her hosts, but Catherine was secretly disappointed. The hall was neat and filled with clean furniture in a modern style. There was no sense of foreboding or misery, and the breeze didn't waft the sighs of murdered ghosts towards her.

'You are most welcome to our home, Miss Morland,' General Tilney said. 'I trust you will be very comfortable with—'

At that moment he removed his watch, glanced at it and declared it was twenty minutes to five. This seemed to shatter the air of calm about them, and Catherine found herself being hurried away by Eleanor in a way that said everything runs like clockwork under the General's strict rules.

'This way, dear friend,' Eleanor said as she led Catherine through an archway and up a wide, oak staircase with many flights and landings. 'Your room is just down here.'

She stopped outside a chamber on the second floor, unlocked the door and gestured for Catherine to step inside.

'Dinner is at five o'clock,' she said, practically whispering. 'Father gets very angry if he's kept waiting. Please don't be long.'

CHAPTER TWENTY-ONE

The room that Catherine now found herself in was nothing like the stories that Henry had told her on the ride to the abbey.

The walls were not draped in dark velvet but were brightly wallpapered and the floor was covered in rich, soft carpet. High windows let in plenty of light and everything had been freshly dusted.

Catherine sighed.

'How lovely this is,' she said to herself, feeling foolish for expecting it to be some haunted cell.

She did not want to keep General Tilney waiting for anything in the world and so quickly set about unwrapping her dresses and changing.

Just as Catherine was about to clamber into a fresh gown for the evening, she spotted something that made her catch her breath in the corner of the room. There, tucked into a deep alcove, was an enormous chest of dark wood and gold gilding.

'What can this be?' she whispered out loud. 'Why should such a strange thing be in my pretty bedroom?'

She edged closer and examined the ancient box with its scrolls and swirls of decoration.

'I must know what's inside.'

Carefully and without making too much noise, Catherine heaved the lid upwards. It was so heavy she could barely budge it, but after a lot of struggling, she managed to lift the cumbersome thing and peek inside.

'Blankets!' she groaned. Disappointed again.

'Can I help you, madam?' a voice suddenly

blurted behind her, and Catherine spun round, dropping the chest's lid with a painfully loud *BANG!* It was Eleanor's maidservant.

'Umm . . . no . . . no, thank you.' Catherine panted. Her heart was beating like a drum in her chest. 'I'm fine.'

The woman bowed her head and exited the way she came, leaving Catherine to come to her senses and quickly scramble into the rest of her clean clothes.

Satisfied, she made a dash for the door and opened it to find Eleanor waiting outside.

'We must hurry,' her friend said with a vexed expression. 'Father will be furious.'

They ran down the stairs together and turned into the drawing room to find General Tilney glaring at his watch and pacing the floor. When he saw the girls, he yanked violently at a bell and hollered, 'Dinner is to be on the table NOW!'

Catherine sat down, trembling and breathless,

and watched quietly as the General's mood gently softened once they were all tucking into their first course. As he relaxed, so did everyone else, and Catherine finally felt brave enough to look around the impressive parlour.

'You must have been used to much bigger dining rooms at Mr Allen's, Miss Morland,' he said when he noticed Catherine looking about.

'No,' she replied politely. 'Mr Allen's parlour wasn't half the size of this. I've never seen such a large room.'

This clearly tickled the General and he smirked contentedly.

Though there was now a heavy storm raging outside, the rest of the evening inside the abbey passed without any other uncomfortable disturbances. On one or two occasions, General Tilney had to leave the room, and there was a definite feeling of relief when he did, but all the same . . . things went smoothly. After more food than Catherine thought possible to eat, she and Eleanor wandered back to their rooms on the second floor as lightning flashed at the window.

'I'm three doors along the hall if you need me,' Eleanor said.

'Good night, sweet friend.' Catherine smiled. She walked into her room and closed the door.

While the Tilneys and their guest had been at dinner, Eleanor's maidservant had been into Catherine's room and built up a delightful fire in the grate. It filled the bedchamber with a warm glow and made everything feel as far from scary and haunted as possible, despite the storm outside.

'How marvellous to find a fire already lit,' she sighed aloud, feeling very spoiled indeed.

It was only after she had put on her nightdress and was about to climb into bed that Catherine noticed something that snatched her attention – a huge cabinet of black wood set into another alcove just like the chest from earlier. How in the world had she missed it before?

She stepped closer to examine the large piece of furniture in the shadows and noticed the key was still in the lock. Hadn't Henry mentioned something when they were journeying here about a dreadful cabinet containing nightmarish things?

'I shall open it,' Catherine whispered to herself as her heart began to thump. 'I'm going to look inside.'

She reached up and turned the lock with a trembling hand as lightning streaked the sky and rain lashed against the windows. At first, the key resisted, but with a grind of rusty metal it eventually twisted with a loud *CLUNK* and the cabinet slowly creaked open.

Behind these first two doors, Catherine found a wall of small drawers all surrounding a second alcove with another locked door.

'Very strange,' she murmured.

Knowing all about such things from her novels, Catherine quickly checked all the tiny drawers, making sure to knock and see if they had false bottoms.

None of them did . . . and they were all . . . empty.

'Whatever horrid secret you conceal,' she

whispered to the cabinet, failing to notice that the fire was beginning to die without her throwing any extra logs on to it, 'must be in your central chamber.'

By now Catherine was trembling all over. She seized the tiny key in the door at the cabinet's heart and turned it. It yielded immediately and in seconds the compartment was open, revealing . . .

'Manuscripts!' Catherine gasped. The fire had grown so dim she could hardly see, but even in the low light it was clear that the papers were covered in looping handwriting. What could they be? Love letters? A scandalous journal from some long-dead relative of the Tilneys? A confession from an evil killer?

All at once, an almighty gust of wind howled down the chimney and extinguished the fire. The room was plunged into total darkness, leaving Catherine standing rigid with fear.

Dropping the papers where she stood, our

heroine made a dive in the direction of the bed, landed safely upon it and scrambled beneath the sheets.

Suddenly everything was filled with horror. The darkness moaned around Catherine as her heart thundered louder than the storm. The curtains of her bed seemed to flap and twitch and the lock on the door rattled. Her blood was chilled by the sound of distant screams and Catherine heard three o'clock proclaimed by all the clocks in the house. Was this the end coming for her? Did she faint after so much dread and terror? Or . . . as she waited for some monster to steal her away . . . did she eventually just drift off to sleep?

We'll never know, my dear reader, but I have a feeling it was the latter . . .

CHAPTER TWENTY-TWO

The sound of the maidservant folding back the window shutters at eight o'clock the next morning was what woke Catherine. She opened one eye and found the room was still where she left it. There was a fresh fire burning in the grate and last night's storm had been replaced by a bright and cheerful morning.

As the maid fussed with the doors on the cabinet and Catherine sat up in bed, she remembered the mysterious manuscripts.

'Leave those!' Catherine bolted out of bed and frantically gathered every scattered sheet from the floor. 'They're just notes from home. I dropped them last night.' She flew back beneath her blankets and waited for the maid to leave before turning to read the tattered papers on her pillow.

This was the moment. Catherine was about to uncover the dark secrets of Northanger Abbey. She took a deep breath and read aloud.

'Shirts, stockings, cravats, waistcoats . . .' Catherine grunted angrily to herself. She snatched the next piece of paper and searched it for some vital clue. 'Hair powder, shoe string, soap for breeches . . .'

The great discovery had been nothing but a bundle of laundry bills and shopping lists!

Feeling more foolish than she'd ever felt in her life, Catherine hurried back out of bed, washed, dressed and headed downstairs to the breakfast parlour. She felt her cheeks blush when she saw Henry sitting at the table, even though he had no idea of the idiotic things she had got up to last night.

'Good morning. I hope the storm didn't disturb you too much?' Henry asked as she sat down opposite him. 'It was a clamorous one.'

'I slept very well,' Catherine mumbled. Even talking about last night seemed to betray her stupidity. She changed the subject. 'But look at what a lovely morning we have now.'

'Quite.' Henry smiled. 'I believe my father wants to show you around the abbey later. I hope that won't bore you.'

'Not at all.' Catherine instantly felt the tingle of excitement again, but she refused to let her mind wander, just for now. 'I should love to explore properly.'

'Marvellous!' A voice spoke behind them. It was General Tilney. He marched into the room, followed by Eleanor. 'I shall enjoy your company on my morning walk, Miss Morland. We can take in the abbey gardens and you can see the whole place properly.'

'Did you sleep well, dear Catherine?' Eleanor asked.

Catherine nodded and pretended to be fascinated by a nearby vase of flowers.

Some time after breakfast, Henry Tilney left for the parsonage at Woodston. Catherine, trying to seem as unsuspicious as possible, wandered over to the parlour windows in the hopes of getting one last glimpse of him as he rode away. She hated to admit it to herself, but she missed him already and wondered when he would return to Northanger Abbey.

As nine o'clock came and went, General Tilney led Catherine and Eleanor out into the gardens at the back of the abbey and a fair distance away from the house.

Catherine was so eager to get a good view of the old place, she didn't much care for the grounds at all, and when they finally rounded a corner near the vegetable troughs and walked out on to the lawns, there it was.

'Goodness!' she exclaimed.

The abbey was far grander and more ornate than she had thought when they approached it from the front yesterday afternoon. The whole building wrapped itself around a large courtyard and it was covered in Gothic ornaments on every corner and buttress.

Catherine had never seen anything like it and the rush of delight that danced about her thoughts was so intense that without waiting for any encouragement, she boldly expressed her amazement of the abbey.

General Tilney was thrilled by Catherine's enthusiasm and grumbled that his own children should show more.

'Next we shall visit the kitchen gardens,' he said. 'Best for miles around.'

'Oh, yes!' Eleanor agreed and made towards a path around the abbey that led through low hanging fir trees.

'No! Not that way,' the General barked at his daughter. 'Why choose that cold, damp path to the gardens? Miss Morland will get wet. It's a terrible place to walk.'

'Sorry, Father,' said Eleanor. 'It's just such a

favourite walk of mine . . .'

Catherine looked down the narrow, winding path and was struck by its gloominess. Eager to enter it, she couldn't stop herself from going to have a look.

'Very well,' the General said, noticing Catherine's interest. 'I shall take the sunny way and meet you both there.'

With that, he turned and walked off to find his alternate route to the kitchen gardens and Catherine was shocked at how relieved she was to see him go.

'This spot is so dear to me,' Eleanor sighed as they walked through the dewy firs. 'It was my mother's favourite walk.'

Catherine suddenly realised she had never heard anyone mention a Mrs Tilney before.

'I used to walk here so often with her, but I never loved it then,' said Eleanor, walking further in. 'Her memory makes it precious to me now, though.'

'Shouldn't her memory make this route precious to your father also?' Catherine dared to ask. 'He refused to enter.'

Eleanor didn't answer the question.

'I was thirteen when she died,' she finally said.

'You must miss her very much,' said Catherine sadly.

'Very much. I have no sister, and though Henry was and still is a great comfort, I do so wish she was here.'

That was it . . . Catherine couldn't help herself. She asked a million questions at once and Eleanor answered as best she could.

In the shortest of times, Catherine gathered that Mrs Tilney had been a beautiful woman with a good and kind heart. She was seemingly very unhappy in her marriage to General Tilney, and Catherine deduced that he must secretly be a very bad man. Now she thought about it, the clues had always been there. How had she not spotted it before? The General's sudden flashes of temper, his overbearing strictness with keeping time and the way Henry and Eleanor behaved like they were almost scared of him. These were all sure signs and it made her feel unexpectedly furious!

'There is a portrait of her . . .' Eleanor mumbled.

'I'd love to see it,' Catherine replied eagerly. 'Where is it? Your father's room?'

'No . . . Father never liked it, so I had it hung in my bedchamber instead,' Eleanor explained. 'I'd be happy to show it to you.'

Catherine couldn't believe what she was hearing! General Tilney had made his wife unhappy, refused to walk her favourite route through the fir trees and didn't want to keep the only portrait of his wife in the family's possession?

The man was a MONSTER!

CHAPTER TWENTY-THREE

The end of the pathway brought them directly to General Tilney, who had been waiting for them and impatiently looking at his watch. In spite of her new belief that he was an absolute villain, Catherine found herself having to nod and smile and listen as politely as she could.

'Shall we begin our tour of the inside?' General Tilney asked once they'd walked the full length of the kitchen gardens three times over.

'Oh, yes!' said Catherine. She was genuinely excited to explore Northanger Abbey's many passageways and she didn't really care about cabbages and carrots, so anything was better than this.

'Very well,' the General said with a little bow. 'Allow me . . .'

He held open a door that entered into a small, dark hallway and from there led Catherine and Eleanor around several corridors until they were back at the foot of the grand, oak staircase.

'Shall we?' He smiled, and the proper tour began.

Catherine tried to take in every detail of the rooms as General Tilney marched through them.

There was a drab drawing room, followed by a useless antechamber with no furniture in it at all, followed by the grandest room Catherine had ever seen. It was the real drawing room – used only when the most important guests came to stay.

'It's so grand!' said Catherine in amazement. She knew absolutely nothing about antiques or styles, but she could certainly see that this was impressive.

Next, they walked through a vaulted library filled with books that made Catherine's knees tremble. She tried a few books on the shelves, but to her sadness, none of them opened a hidden door or triggered a secret trap.

There was the billiard room, the kitchens, Henry's study filled with papers and encyclopaedias and a curious round room with several doors leading off of it. General Tilney informed his guest that this room had once formed part of the cloisters and cells where nuns had lived. Catherine noted with growing curiosity that he didn't open or explain any of the doors and show her what was inside.

'These are our finest bedrooms,' the General continued as they crossed a long gallery with several ornate bedchambers on either side. He listed the famous and regal people who had slept in them in the past with a sense of real pride, and Catherine felt sure he could have gone on for ever if Eleanor had not opened a door at the end of the hall.

'Come back this instant!' he called angrily to his daughter. 'Where do you think you're going?'

'Sorry, Father,' said Eleanor, closing the door, but not before Catherine had seen a narrower winding corridor veering off to one side and the landing of a spiral staircase.

He may not have realised, but by keeping Catherine out of that part of the house, General Tilney had given her the greatest ambition to explore it. What was beyond that large door? Secrets . . . secrets were beyond it!

As they headed back towards the staircase, Eleanor waited until her father was some way ahead before she whispered, 'I was going to show you my mother's room . . . where she died.'

No wonder that horrible gentleman didn't want to go in there!

I bet he's never been back in there, she thought to herself. *His guilt won't allow him!*

The next time Catherine was alone with Eleanor, she plucked up the courage to say how much she'd like to see her mother's old room.

'I'll show it to you when *he* isn't around,' was Eleanor's reply.

'Has it been left just as it was?'

'Yes,' said Eleanor. 'Completely.'

'I suppose you were with her when it happened?'

'No . . .' Eleanor's face fell into sadness. 'I was away from home, and by the time I arrived back, it was all over.'

Catherine's blood turned to ice in her veins as terrible thoughts rushed through her head. *If no one was here but General Tilney, who knows what that villain did to his wife?*

That night after dinner, Catherine climbed into bed and turned the troubled thoughts over and over in her head. The more she puzzled over it, the more she was convinced that the strange, round room with many doors leading from it must have been directly below where Mrs Tilney's old room was. Maybe the spiral staircase was the last place General Tilney dragged his poor wife before locking her up in one of the old nun cells and leaving her to die!

Catherine sneaked out of bed and crept over to

her window. Her bedroom was on the other side of the courtyard to where the round room had been, and she searched the distant windows across the quadrangle for signs of movement or the flicker of a candle.

'Nothing,' she thought out loud.

It must have been too early still. Midnight would be the perfect time to look. That's when General Tilney would be stealing about, for sure. Catherine made a plan to climb out of bed again and take a look at the far windows when the clock struck twelve. She'd catch the General in some ghastly business without fail.

Two hours passed, the clock did indeed strike twelve, and . . . Catherine had been asleep for over thirty minutes.

CHAPTER TWENTY-FOUR

The next day was Sunday and it left Catherine with almost no opportunity to explore. She, Eleanor and every servant were expected to join General Tilney at chapel from the morning all the way through to the afternoon. And as bold as Catherine was feeling, she didn't fancy waiting until the evening and exploring Northanger Abbey by the light of an unreliable candle.

The following day seemed perfect. The two girls dressed early and waited for the General to go on his morning walk before breakfast. This meant that they had the house to themselves and the added bonus of daylight streaming in through every window.

'We'll start here,' Eleanor said, leading Catherine into her bedchamber and pointing out the portrait of Mrs Tilney that they'd spoken about before. 'This is . . . was my mother.'

Catherine looked with a feeling of great sadness at the painted face of a very beautiful woman. There were tiny hints of a likeness with both Henry and Eleanor in her eyes and smile, and she looked like a terribly kind soul.

When they entered the long gallery with the door at the far end leading to Mrs Tilney's bedchamber, both girls were nervous and agitated.

Again, Eleanor unlocked it and they had just slipped inside and were closing the door behind them, when the figure, the DREADFUL figure, of General Tilney appeared at the other end of the gallery.

'Eleanor!' was the only word he barked, and Catherine's blood ran cold. There was a moment when both girls stood in shocked silence until, with an apologetic look at her friend, Eleanor darted out from behind the door and ran to her father.

When the coast was clear and General Tilney had taken Eleanor off to some other part of the house to scream at her, no doubt, Catherine made a dash for it and hid in her room for the rest of the early morning.

Later, tempted by the scent of hot pastries and the sound of gossiping guests, Catherine slipped silently down to the breakfast parlour with her heart pounding in her chest. Was this the moment? Was she about to be shamed and screamed at by the old gentleman for trespassing where she should not have been venturing?

She walked in and saw General Tilney enjoying a cup of tea with a few acquaintances from the local village.

'Ah, Miss Morland,' he said with a smile. 'Do come and join us.'

Catherine was confused and wondered if this was some evil trick to relax her nerves before he struck her with his accusations.

'Don't worry,' Eleanor whispered when General Tilney was busy complaining to a servant that the toast wasn't hot, and the butter was too hard. 'He didn't see you, and he only wanted me to answer a note.'

Catherine could have cried into her breakfast tea to hear those words. Nearly being caught by the General was possibly the most frightening thing to happen yet in this strange place filled with secrets. But she wasn't completely discouraged from trying again . . .

Now the General was entertaining guests, he would be busy right up until dinner time.

Catherine dutifully stayed near General Tilney all day, talking with his friends when he encouraged her to and always staying in sight of him. Then, just before four o'clock, she made her excuses to go and freshen up before dinner.

Poor Eleanor was stuck with her father and his guests, so Catherine would have to go alone. But the daylight would last for at least another hour and she knew the way to Mrs Tilney's bedchamber by now, so her courage held out.

She went up the oak staircase to where her room was on the second floor, but instead of heading in that direction, she turned along the grand gallery and tiptoed to the door at the far end.

'This is it, Catherine,' she said to herself. 'Brace yourself for the horrors that await you.'

Silently, she crept through the door and into the narrow, stone hallway beyond it. There was the spiral staircase descending into the floor as she'd seen before and opposite was a second large door. She crossed the hallway and entered before her nerves could get the better of her.

'Good gracious!' she muttered when she'd opened the second door and stepped inside. 'I don't believe it!'

Catherine found herself standing in a beautiful bedroom, filled with light. It may have remained untouched since Mrs Tilney's death, but the room was as tidy as if the servants had been in there that very morning. The bed was neat, the curtains were drawn, and everything was dappled in late afternoon sun.

A strange feeling bubbled in Catherine's stomach and she knew she'd let her imagination get the better of her for a second time. General Tilney was indeed a hardened man, but he was no monster.

There were no signs of villainy or foul play in this pretty bedchamber. She was entirely wrong and suddenly felt utterly sick at the thought of exploring for one moment longer.

'What a fool you are, Catherine Morland,' she said out loud.

'Are you?'

Catherine yelped and turned as fear quickened her heart. Who had spoken so unexpectedly? She felt a mixture of joy and embarrassment to see Henry standing at the top of the spiral stairs.

'What are you doing in here?' he asked, raising an eyebrow.

'I . . . I . . .' Catherine had never felt so stupid and out of place. 'I wanted to see your mother's room.'

'And was there anything extraordinary to see in there?'

'No. I was just curious. What with her dying so suddenly and none of you around to see it.' Catherine couldn't stop herself. 'And your father . . . I thought he couldn't have been very fond of her and—'

'And you decided my father did something terrible to her?' Henry said. His face was so full of disappointment that it hurt Catherine to look at it. 'My mother died from a cruel sickness. She suffered awful fits for four days and died on the fifth. No one could save her.'

'I didn't know,' Catherine whimpered. 'I just thought there was more to the story and—'

'You thought we were all hiding the secret of my mother's murder!' Henry snapped. 'You think we are living in a novel, Miss Morland! How could you believe something so horrifying of my family? How could you believe it of me?'

'No . . . I . . .'

'What other ideas are in your head?' Henry's eyes welled up and Catherine couldn't bear to watch. With tears now streaking down her cheeks and a feeling of deep shame bubbling in her stomach, she ran off to her room and shut herself inside.

CHAPTER TWENTY-FIVE

All Catherine's secret hopes of romance were dead. Henry's dismay had completely opened her eyes and made her see just how wildly unfair she had been. How would he ever forgive her? She knew the answer . . . he would not.

Catherine cried bitterly to herself and felt such hatred for her own imagination. It suddenly seemed criminal, all her ridiculous accusations of General Tilney.

'What was I thinking?!?' she cried aloud.

By the time the clock struck five, Catherine had worked herself into such a state of misery, she thought it would last for ever. She went downstairs to dinner with a broken heart and could barely string a sentence together when Eleanor asked her if she was well.

To her despair, Henry had stayed for the evening and now she would have to suffer the shame of sitting opposite him while he . . . what would he do? Catherine thought it would be fair if he flung food across the table at her.

'Good evening, Miss Morland,' Henry said with a smile that shocked her to her bones. 'How nice it is to see you.'

Catherine fought back her tears but wanted very much to cry at this. Dear, dear Henry, despite being hurt by Catherine's silly fancies, was being kind to her. He must have realised how dreadful she was feeling and took pity. She had never needed comfort more, and it certainly looked like he was aware of it.

By the end of dinner, as if by some miracle, Catherine was feeling comforted about the situation. Henry's constant smiles and kind words told her that he was not as angry as she had first thought, and she began to relax once more.

Her need for friendly comfort had not vanished altogether though, and for the first time in days, Catherine's mind wandered to Isabella. Why hadn't she written? Before they parted ways in Bath, Isabella had promised to write very regularly, and she had never broken a promise before.

The mornings came and went and with them the daily post. Every day Catherine would watch for some note or letter with news in it, but nothing ever arrived. That was until nine days passed.

Finally, after washing and dressing, Catherine headed into the breakfast parlour to find Henry standing just inside the door with an envelope in his hand.

'For you, Miss Morland,' he said with a mischievous grin.

'Oh! Finally.' Catherine beamed as she took it. 'I've been waiting for . . . oh . . . this is a letter from James.'

A feeling of dread crept into her thoughts as she opened and unfolded the note. She read carefully with trembling fingers.

Dear Catherine,

God knows I didn't want to be writing this, but I knew you'd be anxious to hear any news and it is my duty to tell you. Everything is at an end between Isabella and I. I left her and Bath yesterday, and I hope never to see either again. She has made me miserable for ever and given her heart to Frederick Tilney instead of me. They are to be married.

I wish I'd never met her!

Take care, my dear sister. Be careful who you fall in love with.

James

Catherine had only made it to the third line of James's letter before she began to heave little sobs. Henry and Eleanor, seeing that their friend could only be receiving bad news, quickly escorted her out into the hall before General Tilney caught wind of the commotion and demanded to know what was wrong.

'Catherine, my friend,' Eleanor whispered. 'Whatever is it? I hope it is not bad news from Fullerton? Your mother or father?'

'No,' Catherine replied with fresh tears pouring from her eyes. 'The note is from my brother James, in Oxford.'

'Miss Morland, what's happened? We don't want to pry into other people's business, but do tell us,' said Henry.

'That's just it . . .' Catherine wept. 'It is your business as well as mine.'

'I don't understand,' Henry said, looking more and more concerned with each passing second.

'Isabella has broken James's heart and has now declared her love for your brother instead.'

'Frederick!' Eleanor gasped.

'They are to be married,' said Catherine through her sobs. 'Poor James!'

'I am shocked,' Henry blurted. 'That doesn't sound like Frederick at all. Is Miss Thorpe certain she hasn't made a mistake?'

'How could she?' Catherine asked.

'I can believe that Isabella would be unfaithful to James and I absolutely believe that James must be heartbroken, but there's no way Frederick would want to get married. He's just not the type.'

'Well if Isabella has lost James for a man she mistakenly thinks wants to marry her, she's going to regret it indeed,' Catherine mused. 'Do you know, for a tiny second, I was terribly sad to realise I've lost Isabella too. But, now . . . now I think I miss her less than I thought I did.'

CHAPTER TWENTY-SIX

Over the coming days, Isabella and Frederick were all that Catherine, Eleanor and Henry could talk about. They passed the hours guessing and wondering at what the sorry pair might be doing, whether they were still in love, and if Frederick would ever write to the General for permission to wed his future bride.

'I don't think he'll ever have the courage to ask Father,' Eleanor said, trying to hide her annoyance at her eldest brother.

'Ask Father what?' General Tilney grumbled as he strode into the breakfast parlour.

'Nothing,' Henry lied with a smile. 'We were

discussing a character in one of Miss Morland's books.'

'Hmm,' came the General's reply.

The days rolled on further and Catherine was terribly saddened when Henry had to leave for Woodston to carry out his parson's duties. But where there was loss, there was gain, as on Sunday afternoon General Tilney decided it would be a very good idea for him, Catherine and Eleanor to take a day trip.

'On Wednesday, I say we take a carriage and visit Woodston,' he said. 'I think you will find the parsonage charming, Miss Morland. What do you say?'

'Visit Henry?' Catherine said, her spirits brightening immediately.

'Indeed.'

'I should love it!' And love it she did.

***

Catherine worried that Wednesday would be wet and that they'd have to cancel the trip, but thankfully when the day arrived, it was as bright and sunny a day as she could have asked for. Along with General Tilney and Eleanor, she took a carriage just after breakfast and made the twenty-mile journey to Henry's parsonage in Woodston.

'Oh! It's so charming,' is all Catherine could repeat as they clattered into the streets of the bustling village after a very bumpy two-hour journey.

Henry was already waiting at the gates of his home when the carriage arrived, and Catherine felt lighter than air to see him. She was nothing but smiles as they spent the afternoon walking around the grounds, catching up on gossip and playing with Henry's four dogs. Catherine felt certain that this was the nicest day of her life so far, and even General Tilney seemed in a marvellous mood. He was as cheerful as she'd ever seen him, smiling and

nodding every time he watched Catherine and Henry talking together.

At four o'clock, they all sat down to an early dinner and by six o'clock it was time to begin the journey back. Catherine felt hollow at the thought

of leaving Henry again. His little home in Woodston was more lovely than anything she could see in Bath, and she spent the journey back to Northanger Abbey worrying terribly about when she would see it and him again.

CHAPTER TWENTY-SEVEN

Catherine's worrying was short-lived. When they arrived back at the abbey, she was greeted with something that very quickly made her forget about everything else. A letter from Isabella . . .

My dearest Catherine,

I received your two letters with the greatest delight, and I'm terribly sorry for not replying sooner.

Thank goodness we leave this vile city tomorrow. Since you went away, Bath has been incredibly dull. Everyone I care about has left and I get no pleasure from being here any more.

I'm very worried as I haven't heard from James since he returned to Oxford and I fear there may have been some kind of misunderstanding. I know you can fix it. He is the only man I have ever loved, and I trust you to convince him of it, dear friend.

Spring fashions are in the shops now and they're very boring. The hats are frightful!

I hope you're having fun with the Tilneys. I must say I'm so glad that Frederick has left Bath. I hate him! You remember he always wanted my attention? Remember he was always looking for me? Well, he soon turned his attention to Charlotte Davis! I didn't mind of course.

Do tell me about James. I was worried that he seemed a little strange when he left. Did he have a cold? I'm very unhappy about it. I'd write to him myself, but I have lost his address. I know you'll do it for me, dearest.

Anne Mitchell tried to wear a dress exactly like mine at the theatre the other night. She looked dreadful, although I looked wonderful in it. At least that's what Frederick Tilney said.

Please write to James for me. Waste no time.

Isabella

Such a lot of lies could not even appeal to Catherine's kind heart. The letter was full of them! It was stuffed with falseness and inconsistencies right from the first line.

A strange feeling crept over Catherine as she read Isabella's words and she realised that she was ashamed of her, and ashamed for ever being her friend.

'Write to James for you?' she said to the letter as if it were Isabella herself. 'No! He will never hear your name again!'

When Henry finally visited Northanger Abbey again, Catherine was eager to tell him all about the news of his brother.

'He ran off with Charlotte Davis?' Henry said, looking thoughtful. 'Do you know, I don't think he ever loved Isabella.'

'Neither do I,' Eleanor agreed.

'Do you think Frederick only did it out of mischief?' Catherine asked.

Henry nodded.

'Then I think Isabella is even more foolish for believing him. She was only searching for money and finery.'

Catherine decided at that moment that she would not reply to the letter. Poor James deserved any attention Catherine had to spare, and Isabella deserved none of it.

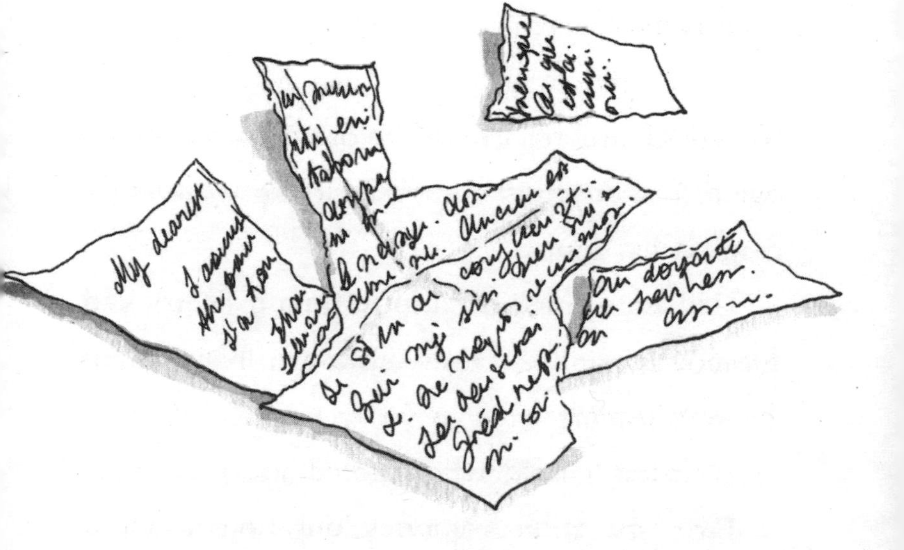

CHAPTER TWENTY-EIGHT

Soon after their day trip to Woodston, General Tilney had to leave Northanger Abbey for a week of important meetings in London.

'Make sure you see to Miss Morland at all hours,' he ordered Henry before he set off. 'Her comfort is the most important thing.' And with that, he was gone . . .

Catherine didn't need to admit it to Henry and Eleanor as she knew they felt it too, but General Tilney's leaving gave her a feeling of calm and relief. It was like the whole house breathed out.

From that moment, everything became a joy. The three of them laughed and relaxed together, they walked where they liked when they liked, mealtimes were full of chatter, and a sense of ease filled the many rooms and corridors of the abbey.

Henry couldn't stick to his father's rules entirely as he had to return to Woodston for a sermon he was giving, but he promised to return straight back in two days.

Without the stress of having the General around, Catherine felt far easier about Henry going away for a little while, and she looked forward to spending some time alone with Eleanor.

But . . .

That night after a very late dinner, the two girls were about to head to the drawing room for a game of cards when they spotted a horse and carriage clattering its way up the driveway towards the house. It was clear that whoever was riding it was in a rush to reach the abbey.

'Who could that be?' Eleanor said. She peered through the window then suddenly gasped and spun round to face Catherine. 'It must be Frederick!'

'I don't want to see him!' Catherine blurted. 'Not after what happened to James.'

'Go!' Eleanor said, pointing to the staircase. 'Return to your room and I shall deal with my foolish brother. I'll come to you when it is done.'

With that, Catherine dashed upstairs and closed her bedroom door behind her. She listened carefully, hoping to catch a word or two, but she was now too far away from the entrance hall and could only hear a distant man's voice. He was shouting and was clearly very angry.

After five minutes, whatever conversation had been taking place downstairs was over, and there was only silence beyond the bedroom door.

'What should I do now?' Catherine whispered to herself, before becoming aware of the sound of soft footsteps outside in the hall.

They came closer and closer, until . . . someone was right outside her bedroom. Catherine held her breath and watched as the door handle moved slightly. Her skin prickled with goosebumps and the hair on the back of her neck tingled.

Could it be Frederick? Whoever it was, somebody had their hand on the other side of the handle and—

'Yes?' Refusing to let her imagination run away with her like it had done in the past, Catherine opened the door and greeted the stranger in the hall.

It was Eleanor, only Eleanor.

Catherine smiled for a moment, but then quickly frowned. Something was wrong. Eleanor's face was ghostly pale, and she was visibly shaking.

'What is it?' she asked, taking Eleanor by the hand and leading her to the edge of the bed. 'Whatever has happened?'

'Oh, Catherine,' Eleanor finally managed to say. 'I come to you with such frightful news.'

'Is Frederick all right?'

'It was not my brother,' Eleanor whimpered.

Catherine's heart skipped a beat. 'Something has happened to Henry!?'

'No.' Eleanor took Catherine's hands and looked deeply into her eyes. 'My father has returned from London early.'

'General Tilney?'

'Oh, Catherine, what I'm about to tell you is so horrible, but you must know I'm only the messenger. I would not want this to happen for all the world.'

'What?' Catherine's heart was practically in her throat. 'My dear friend, please say, I cannot last a moment longer.'

'My father has returned from London in a terrible rage. He will not say why, but he demands that you are to leave Northanger Abbey.'

Catherine jolted in shock.

'He has arranged a carriage to come for you at sunrise and will not allow you to stay a moment longer. I'm so sorry, my friend. If I had my way, you'd stay for ever.'

There was a long silence as Catherine's mind raced. General Tilney must have found out about her wild accusations to do with Mrs Tilney. He must be so furious with her. Catherine could hardly blame him.

'It is my fault,' she said, fighting back tears.

'It is cruelty!' Eleanor sobbed. 'To cast you out like this. You have been such a delight to have here at the abbey and now this is how my father treats you.'

'I deserve it,' said Catherine. She felt as cold and hard as a stone at that moment. 'It won't be so bad. One of your father's servants can accompany me to Salisbury, I'm sure, and then I am only nine miles from home. We can write and you can come to Fullerton to visit whenever you like.'

'No,' Eleanor cried. 'Father says no one is to accompany you on the journey. You have to find your own way. I am forbidden to write or see you again, Catherine. I HATE HIM!'

Catherine could hear no more and politely asked her friend to leave.

'I shall see you in the morning,' said Eleanor, pulling Catherine into a tight hug. 'I'm so sorry. My father is a wicked man after all.'

***

Daylight came and Catherine was already dressed and packed to leave. She had spent the whole night awake and crying and was now filled with such a sense of shame, she couldn't even be angry at General Tilney. *This is what happens to silly little girls who read novels*, she thought.

Downstairs she found Eleanor waiting for her near the open front door, looking miserable and dejected. The carriage was waiting just outside.

'You will need this for your journey,' she whispered and slipped a small pouch of money into Catherine's hand. 'Father didn't want me to give you any.'

Catherine smiled at her sweet friend and felt terribly guilty. This was all her fault.

'Please say goodbye to Henry for me.'

'I will, my dear Catherine. I promise.'

There were no further words. With tears streaming down her face, Catherine stepped into the carriage and left Northanger Abbey behind her.

CHAPTER TWENTY-NINE

Catherine was too wretched to be worried about making the long journey to Fullerton by herself. She huddled in the corner of the General's carriage and couldn't even bring herself to look back at the abbey as it vanished into the distance.

Eventually, the coach reached Salisbury. Catherine had spotted the tall spire of its cathedral as they approached from several miles away and felt a great uneasiness as they got closer. When they reached the market square, she was told by the driver that this was as far as he was permitted to take her. She politely stepped down from her seat without complaining or fussing and was soon left completely alone.

From there on, Catherine had to rely on trustworthy signposts to point her in the right direction and inform her which carriages to take as she hopped from village to village, edging her way home. And after eleven hours of tiresome travel, she found herself entering the familiar village of Fullerton.

Now, I know what you're thinking. You think that heroines are supposed to return home after a grand adventure, rich beyond their wildest dreams or glittering with the love of a nation. You think there should be trumpet fanfares and parades and feasting for weeks to come, and here we are bringing our heroine home in misery and disgrace.

Well, the story isn't quite over just yet . . .

A horse and carriage was a rare sight in the sleepy little village, so the whole family were at the window when Catherine arrived at the gates.

Her father, mother and siblings Sarah, George and Harriet all assembled at the door to welcome

Catherine home and as they hugged and cheered, she felt a twinkle of happiness. She hadn't expected to ever feel it again but being suddenly surrounded by love calmed her nerves and lessened the despair in her heart.

'Tell us everything,' Mrs Morland said after whisking her daughter indoors for a cup of tea. Mothers can always tell when their children are upset, and there was no way Catherine was going to get away without explaining everything that had led her back to Fullerton so unexpectedly.

Catherine tried her best. She told the story honestly and with every detail she could remember, while Mr and Mrs Morland listened with wrinkled brows.

'That General Tilney has no honour!' Mr Morland snapped when Catherine had finished.

'It's a strange business, and he must be a very strange man,' agreed Mrs Morland. She leant in and kissed her daughter on the forehead. 'I can see you're giving yourself all sorts of stress trying to understand it, Catherine, but some things are not worth understanding. You're home now.'

Catherine was left to unpack her bag and begin her life at home all over again. She tried to write a letter to Eleanor but was far too upset and didn't want to get her into trouble with General Tilney. Instead, she returned the money Eleanor had lent her with a note saying only *Thank you, and a thousand good wishes from a most affectionate heart.*

It was alarming how quickly life turned back to normal in Fullerton. Catherine helped around the house, repaired clothes and read books whenever she could. She even joined her mother on a trip to the bottom of the lane to see Mr and Mrs Allen, who had now returned from Bath.

'I really have not patience with the General,' Mrs Allen grumbled again and again after hearing the news. She was quite furious at how he'd treated

Catherine until her mind wandered and she spent the rest of the afternoon talking about her dresses.

'Don't be sad,' Mrs Morland said kindly as they walked home later that day. Then she joked, 'No one in Bath will invite you to dance again if you're grumpy.'

Catherine laughed. She walked through the garden gate, looked up and there she met the eyes of none other than Henry Tilney . . .

***

Upon arriving home and finding him standing on their garden path, Mrs Morland had insisted that Henry came in for a cup of tea. Catherine's brothers and sisters had asked him a thousand questions and he'd answered them all with a good nature. There had been cake and talk of Bath with Mr Morland, but now . . . finally . . . Catherine's parents had given them permission to take a walk together.

'Catherine!' Henry said when they were alone at last. 'I came as soon as I heard what my horrible father had done to you!' He looked at her and she felt like she could float away. 'Father was furious when I told him I was going to travel to Fullerton, but I don't care. I don't think I shall ever speak to him, nor him to me again. I love you, Miss Morland!'

Catherine let out a laugh of total happiness.

'I have loved you since we danced together,' he continued.

'And I love you,' Catherine replied. She wasn't about to be polite and wait for him to kiss her after all this time, so she took his face in her hands and kissed him first.

Everything was marvellous . . .

CHAPTER THIRTY

So, there you have it, my dear reader.

Miss Morland found love with a very worthy gentleman indeed and she had the grandest of adventures along the way.

It turned out that General Tilney hadn't known of Catherine's wild ideas about him being a murderer at all. No . . . his unfair rage had simply been because he found out she wasn't as rich as he thought she was.

John Thorpe was to blame. You remember the night at the theatre, when Catherine had seen him talking to General Tilney? Well, it just so happens that the General had asked John all about Catherine.

At that time, John was convinced that he was going to marry her and being the boastful little toad that he is, he lied and said she was extremely rich, all to try to impress the General.

Later, when General Tilney had visited London, he ran into John at the Bedford Club and the brute, now angry at Catherine for rejecting him, lied again and said she was practically a pauper!

The General was so furious he . . . well, you know the rest.

Eleanor Tilney also found love with a handsome viscount who came to stay at the abbey and she finally escaped her lonely life in Gloucestershire. The General, filled with joy at Eleanor's happiness and at the prospect of welcoming a rich new son-in-law to the family, forgave Henry and gave his blessing for him to marry Catherine.

The pair were married at Northanger Abbey

itself. Bells rang, drinks flowed, and everyone was very, very happy.

I suppose the message of this tale, if it has one at all, is that love does not come from being quiet or docile, well-to-do or empty-headed, pretty or

poised. No . . . love comes from a delicious mix of wild fancies, too many books, friendships, tyranny, kindness, tantrums, beating hearts, foolishness, tenderness, looking at the world with sparkling eyes, laughing until you cry and lots and lots of disobedience . . .

A NOTE FROM STEVEN

The very fact that you're holding this book in your hands means you're doing much better than I ever did when it comes to Jane Austen.

I believe honesty is the best policy and it's time to tell the truth. I, Steven Butler, didn't read an Austen novel until I was thirty-seven years old. ANCIENT!

When the lovely people at Hachette Children's Group asked me to retell *Northanger Abbey*, I was filled with a mixture of excitement and pant-wetting terror. What if it was too difficult? What if I couldn't do it? What if it was too (whispers the next word) boring?

Thankfully, none of these things turned out to be true. I leapt off the deep end, diving headfirst into Jane Austen's world and was amazed at how brilliant her stories are. Plot twists and eccentric characters are in abundant supply . . . and they're funny! I had no idea just how funny Miss Austen's books were going to be.

To cut a long story short, I fell completely in love with *Northanger Abbey* over the course of reading it (ten times!) and rewriting it. Poor Catherine Morland tries so hard to be good, but her unbelievable knack for getting into trouble or doing the wrong thing was what instantly appealed to me. She's so curious and accident-prone but, ultimately, she's kind, and I think that's a very underrated quality. I hope I'm a bit like Catherine . . .

If you've ever read a Steven Butler book, you'll know that there's always a thread of mischief that's woven into my stories, so I loved the impishness of this one. You may disagree, but I think *Northanger Abbey* is a book that pretends to be all about keeping to the rules when secretly it's all about breaking them. There's a reason the last word of the novel is 'disobedience' and I think it's marvellous.

I feel stupid for not picking up a Jane Austen novel earlier in life. I would have loved to experience these stories when I was growing up, I just didn't know it at the time.

So, give yourself a pat on the back. You've finished *Northanger Abbey*, you clever thing, and may your life be filled with wild adventures, daring escapes and lots of love . . . just like Catherine Morland.

A NOTE FROM ÉGLANTINE

My name is Églantine Ceulemans, and as you might have noticed thanks to my first name . . . I am French!

In France, we tend to associate Britain with wonderful English gardens, a unique sense of humour, William Shakespeare and, last but not least, Jane Austen!

It was such an honour to have the opportunity

to illustrate Jane Austen's stories. I have always enjoyed reading books that are filled with love, laughter and happy endings, and Austen writes all of those things brilliantly. And who wouldn't love to illustrate gorgeous dresses, stunning mansions and passionate young women standing up for their deep convictions? I also tried to do justice to Austen's humour and light-heartedness by drawing characterful people and adding in friendly pets (sometimes well-hidden and always witnessing intense but mostly funny situations!).

I discovered Jane Austen's work with *Pride and Prejudice* one sun-filled summer, and I have such good memories of sitting reading it in the garden beneath my grandmother's weeping willow. This setting definitely helped me to fall in love with the book, but it would be a lie to say that I wasn't moved by Elizabeth and Mr Darcy's love story and that I didn't laugh when her mother tried (with no shame at all) to marry her daughters to all the best catches in the town! I imagined all those characters in my head so vividly, and it was a real pleasure to finally illustrate them, alongside all Austen's other amazing characters.

Jane Austen is an author who managed to depict nineteenth-century England with surprising modernity. She questioned the morality of so-called well-to-do people and she managed to write smartly, sharply and independently, at a time where women were considered to be nothing if not married to a man. I hope that these illustrated versions of her books will help you to question the past and the present, without ever forgetting to laugh . . . and to dream!

SO, WHO WAS JANE AUSTEN?

Jane Austen was born in 1775 and had seven siblings. Her parents were well-respected in their local community, and her father was the clergyman for a nearby parish. She spent much of her life helping to run the family home, whilst reading and writing in her spare time.

JANE AUSTEN

Jane began to anonymously publish her work in her thirties and four of her novels were released during her lifetime: *Sense and Sensibility*, *Pride and Prejudice*, *Mansfield Park* and *Emma*. However, at the age of forty-one she became ill, eventually dying in 1817. Her two remaining novels, *Northanger Abbey* and *Persuasion*, were published after her death.

Austen's books are well-known for their comedy, wit and irony. Her observations about wealthy society, and especially the role women played in it, were unlike anything that had been published before. Her novels were not widely read or praised until years later, but they have gone on to leave a mark on the world for ever, inspiring countless poems, books, plays and films.

AND WHAT WAS IT LIKE IN 1817?

WAS READING A POPULAR PASTIME?

Like Catherine Morland, many people who lived during the Regency era and who were from educated backgrounds enjoyed reading. During the 18th and 19th centuries, libraries were set up which made books accessible to many more people. Being a member of a library wasn't free, but it made reading for pleasure much more affordable – since buying your own copy of a book could cost almost £100 in today's money! Libraries were also seen as popular places to socialise, so they were always busy.

At the time, there were many genres for people to choose from, but Gothic novels were particularly popular. These types of novels were filled with horror, mystery and often the supernatural.

Catherine is a fan of this genre as we see from her fascination with *The Mysteries of Udolpho* – a Gothic novel published in 1794 by Ann Radcliffe.

WAS IT COMMON FOR PEOPLE TO GO ABROAD?

It was nowhere near as simple or quick to travel abroad during the Regency era as it is today; passenger trains did not become widespread until later in the 19th century and working aeroplanes were not built until the 20th century. As a result, in 1817, it was mainly men from wealthy backgrounds who went overseas, either for business or education purposes. The most popular destination was France as it was the easiest place to get to by boat from England. This helps to explain why Henry is surprised when he thinks Catherine has travelled to France. However, we're quickly told she's never travelled abroad and that her knowledge of France only comes from books.

WHY DID PEOPLE VISIT THE BATH ASSEMBLY ROOMS?

During the Regency era, Bath was a popular destination. It was seen as a fashionable city where the rich spent their time socialising and enjoying themselves. One of the reasons for its popularity was the Bath Assembly Rooms – a building in the centre of Bath that hosted balls and other events. Balls were held here twice a week and attracted as many as 1,200 guests a night (no wonder Catherine and Mrs Allen complain about the crowds!). This gave young men and women the opportunity to meet people from outside their social circles and develop relationships that would not be allowed otherwise, as we see between Henry and Catherine. The Bath Assembly Rooms also contained rooms for visitors to play card games or gamble, rooms for refreshments and meals and rooms for people to enjoy live music.

WHY DID PEOPLE VISIT THE GRAND PUMP ROOM?

Bath is a city famous for its thermal waters and in the late 17th century, people began to drink these waters believing that they brought them good health. In 1706, the first Pump Room was completed but over the years the popularity of this practice grew and so the Pump Room was extended and became known as the Grand Pump Room. People during the Regency era would visit to drink the waters but mainly it was used as a place to socialise with other guests – it was common practice for people to parade up and down the room, chatting and gossiping. This is where Catherine and Isabella first meet and from there their friendship grows.

COLLECT THEM ALL!

AWESOMELY AUSTEN
JANE AUSTEN'S
PERSUASION
WITTY WORDS BY NARINDER DHAMI
DELIGHTFUL DOODLES BY ÉGLANTINE CEULEMANS

AWESOMELY AUSTEN
JANE AUSTEN'S
SENSE AND SENSIBILITY
WITTY WORDS BY JOANNA NADIN
DELIGHTFUL DOODLES BY ÉGLANTINE CEULEMANS

AWESOMELY AUSTEN
JANE AUSTEN'S
MANSFIELD PARK
WITTY WORDS BY AYISHA MALIK
DELIGHTFUL DOODLES BY ÉGLANTINE CEULEMANS